SNAPSHOT

Also by Brandon Sanderson from Gollancz:

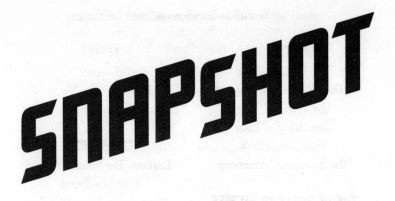

SNAPSHOT

BRANDON SANDERSON®

GOLLANCZ

LONDON

First published in Great Britain in 2018 by Gollancz
an imprint of the Orion Publishing Group Ltd
Carmelite House, 50 Victoria Embankment
London EC4Y 0DZ

An Hachette UK Company

1 3 5 7 9 10 8 6 4 2

A CIP catalogue record for this book is
available from the British Library.

ISBN (Hardback) 978 1 473 22499 5
ISBN (eBook) 978 1 473 22500 8

Printed in Great Britain by Clays Ltd, Elcograf S.p.A.

www.brandonsanderson.com
www.gollancz.co.uk

Acknowledgments

Getting a story to readers involves more than just my writing it. There's a large group working behind the scenes to make sure the entire book is beautiful and polished.

Thanks go to Peter Orullian and Steve Diamond, who took great care to make *Snapshot* awesome in every way. As always, Moshe Feder, Joshua Bilmes, and the indisputable Peter Ahlstrom gave excellent editorial notes, and the story is better because of it. Deanna Hoak did a great job with the copyedit, and the talented Howard Lyon is responsible for the beautiful cover illustration.

Huge appreciation goes out to the community of early readers, whose feedback was invaluable. Trae Cooper, Mark Lindberg, Nikki Ramsay, Ted Herman, Gary Singer, Ross Newberry, Alice Arneson, Louis Hill, Bob Kluttz, Lyndsey Luther, Megan Kanne, Brian T. Hill, Richard Fife, Ben Black, Aubree Pham, Bao Pham, Josh Walker, Jory Phillips, and Eric Lake. I'd particularly like to thank Lora Jean Buss and Glen Buss for their law enforcement feedback, and Kristina Kugler for her proofreading help.

Once again my team at Dragonsteel read the story, provided early feedback, and continue to support me and my books in every way possible. Peter Ahlstrom, Karen Ahlstrom, Kara Stewart, Isaac Stewart, Adam Horne, and Emily Sanderson.

One

Anthony Davis—one of only two real people in a city of twenty million—caught the burrito his partner tossed to him. "Which end is the mustard on?" he asked.

"Mustard?" Chaz replied. "Who puts mustard on a burrito?"

"You. What side?"

Chaz grinned, showing perfect white teeth. They were fake. After taking that bar stool to the face two years back, he'd gotten one replaced, but had insisted that the dentist make it too perfect to match his other teeth. By this point, he'd had most of the rest replaced as well.

"Mustard is in the end on your left," Chaz said, nodding to the burrito. "How'd you know?"

Davis just grunted, ripping off the corner of the burrito. Beans, cheese, beef. And *mustard*. Chaz clung to this stupid belief that someday his partner would happen upon a mustardy bite and convert. Davis shook his head and tossed the ripped-off chunk of burrito into a dumpster.

The two strolled down the street in plain clothes. The vast city of New Clipperton enveloped them, so authentic that one would never be able to tell it was a Snapshot—a re-creation of a specific day in the real city. Using methods a simple cop like Davis struggled to understand, the entire city had been reproduced.

They were actually in some vast underground complex, but it didn't seem that way to him; he saw a sun overhead and smelled the stench of the alleyway they passed. It all felt real to him. In its way, it *was* real: built from raw matter you could touch, smell, hear, and—as evidenced by the bite Davis took of his burrito—taste.

Damn. He'd missed some of the mustard.

"You ever wonder," Chaz said, talking with his mouth half-full, "how much these burritos cost? Like, for real. The energy to create them and stick them in here so we can buy them?"

"They cost tons," Davis said, then took another bite. "And nothing at the same time."

"Huh. Kind of like how you can say things, but have them mean nothing at the same time?"

"The Snapshot Project is a sunk cost, Chaz," Davis said. "The suits already paid for the place, the technology to do this. Everything is already here, and the setup cost was enormous. But we didn't really have much choice."

When the new American government had pulled out of Clipperton, they'd decided not to remove the installation built underneath it. Davis had always assumed that the Americans wanted the place to stay around, in case they decided to return and play with their experiment some more. But they also hadn't wanted to just *give* it away. So, New Clipperton—officially an independent city-state—had been granted the "opportunity" to take control of the Snapshot Project. For a very large fee.

Davis took another bite of his burrito. "This whole thing cost us a ton, but that's done. So we might as well use it."

"Yeah, but burritos, man. They make burritos for us. I always wondered if the bean counters would figure, 'Burritos are too frivolous. Let's take them out.'"

"Doesn't work that way. If you're going to use the Snapshot to re-create a day, you have to do it exactly. So our burritos, the graffiti on the wall there, the woman you're leering at— all part of the package. Expensive, but free, all at once."

"She *is* fine though, eh?" Chaz said, turning around and walking backward as he watched the woman.

"Have a little decency, Chaz."

"Why? She's not real. None of them are real."

Davis took another bite of burrito. His taste buds couldn't

tell that it wasn't real. Of course, what did it mean to be "real"? The beans and cheese had been modeled on a real burrito in the real city, and it was exact down to the molecular level. It wasn't just some virtual simulation either. If you'd placed this burrito beside one from the real world, even an electron microscope couldn't have detected the difference.

Chaz grunted, biting into his own burrito. "Wonder who bought these in the real city."

It was a good question. This Snapshot had been created overnight, and was an exact replica of a day ten days back: the first of May, 2018. This entire re-creation would be deleted once Chaz and Davis left for the evening. They'd push a button, and everything in here would be reconstituted back to raw matter and energy.

Chaz and Davis were real though—from "in real life," so to speak. Their insertion—while necessary—was also problematic. As Chaz and Davis interacted with the Snapshot, they would cause what were called Deviations: differences between the Snapshot and the way the real May first had played out.

Some things they did—though it was impossible to tell which ones ahead of time—would end up having a ripple effect throughout the Snapshot, making the re-creation happen differently from the real day. The Deviation percentage—as calculated by statisticians—would be a factor in any trials associated with evidence discovered in the Snapshot.

Chaz and Davis usually left that to the bean counters. Sometimes, they'd go the entire day doing things they were sure would ruin their cases—but in the end everything played out fine, and the Deviation percentage was determined to be small. Another time, Davis had locked himself away in a hotel saferoom, determined not to create any Deviations. Unfortunately, by slamming his door, he'd woken up a woman in an adjacent room. She had therefore made it to an interview on time, and that had sent ripples throughout the entire Snapshot, causing a 20 percent Deviation level. That had cost them an entire case.

Nobody had blamed him. Cops in the Snapshot would introduce Deviations; it was the nature of what they did. Still, it haunted him. In here, everyone else was fake, but he and Chaz . . . They were somehow something worse. Flaws in a perfect system. Intruders. Viruses leaving chaos in their wakes.

It doesn't matter, he told himself as he finished the last of the burrito. *Eyes on the mission.* The department shrink told him to focus on what he was doing, on his task at hand. He couldn't function if he fixated on the Deviations.

The two made their way to the corner of Third and Twenty-Second, near rows of little shops. Convenience stores, a liquor shop with bars on the windows. The backs of the stop signs had random stickers from this band or that plastered over them. This wasn't one of the nicer areas of the city; there weren't many of those left.

Davis called up the mission parameters again on his phone, looking them over. "I think we should stand inside," Davis said, gesturing toward the liquor store.

"Makes it hard to chase someone."

"Yeah, but he won't see us. No Deviations."

"Deviations can't be stopped."

He was right. Each day, they'd be interviewed about what they did, and data from their phones—which tracked their location—would be downloaded. Their actions were audited by the bean counters in IA, but the language was always about "minimizing Deviation risk in targets." Never about *eliminating* the Deviations.

Besides, the phone data could be fudged, as Davis well knew, and signals from outside had trouble reaching inside the Snapshot. So really, nobody knew for sure what they did in here.

Still, Chaz didn't argue further as Davis positioned them inside the liquor store, which was open despite the early hour. The place smelled clean, and was well maintained, notwithstanding the unsavory section of town. A bearded Sikh man with a sharp red turban swept the floor by the checkout counter. He regarded them curiously as they set up near the front window.

Davis read the mission parameters again, then checked his watch. A half hour. Not much time. They shouldn't have stopped for breakfast, despite Chaz's complaining.

The shopkeeper continued his sweeping, eyeing them periodically.

"He's going to be trouble," Chaz noted.

"We're just two normal patrons."

"Who didn't buy anything. Now we're staring out the window, one of us checking his watch every fifteen seconds."

"I'm not—"

Davis was interrupted as the shopkeeper finally set his broom aside and came walking over. "I'm going to need you to leave," he said. "I need to close for, um, lunch."

Davis smiled, preparing a lie to placate the man.

Chaz flashed his badge.

It looked normal to Davis. Just a silvery shield with the usual important-looking embossing. Nothing abnormal about it. Except it was a reality badge. To anyone from the Snapshot—to anyone who was a dupe, a fake person—it wouldn't look like a normal police shield at all. Instead, it was certification that the men bearing it were real.

And equally, certification that *you* were *not*.

The Sikh man stared at the badge, eyes widening. Davis

always wondered what it was they saw. They got that same far-off look in their eyes, as if they'd stared into something vast. Stunned. Even a little in awe.

Has a dupe of me ever seen one of those? he wondered. *Thinking he was the real me, completely ignorant of the fact that he—and his entire world—was just a Snapshot. Until he saw the badge . . .*

The shopkeeper shook himself and looked at them. "Hey, that's a neat trick. How did you . . . I mean, how'd you make it . . ." He trailed off, looking down at the badge again.

Dupes always recognized it instinctively. Something inside them knew what the badge meant, even if they hadn't ever heard about them. Of course, most *had* heard of them, with the privacy dustups recently. Beyond that, the general public up in the Restored American Union had a fascination with the project; it was becoming a favorite of cinema. You could stream half a dozen cop dramas about detectives working inside a Snapshot—though as far as Davis knew, the only official facility was here in New Clipperton.

The cop dramas never showed what the reality badge looked like. It seemed to be some kind of unwritten rule. It was better in your head.

The shopkeeper whispered something softly in his native tongue. Then he looked up at them again, more somber. Chaz nodded to him.

The shopkeeper took it well. He just . . . wandered off. He pushed out the door of his shop in a daze, leaving it all behind. Why work a retail job when you've just found out you aren't real? Why bother with anything when your entire world is going to end around bedtime?

"Want anything to drink?" Chaz asked cheerfully as he tucked his badge into his front pocket. He nodded to the now-unguarded store shelves.

"You didn't need to do that," Davis said.

"We only have a few minutes left. No time for chitchat. This was the best way."

"He'll introduce Deviations."

"There's no way to stop—"

"Shut it," Davis said, slumping against the window and checking his watch again. *Sometimes I hate you, Chaz.*

Though he envied Chaz at the same time. Davis would be better off if he could simply start viewing everything in here—even the people they passed—as fake. Puppets created from raw matter and animated for a short time.

It was just that . . . they were *exact* reproductions, right down to their brain chemistry. How could you not view them as real people? He and Chaz ate the burritos, treated *them* as real, but were at the same time supposed to pretend the people they met were nothing more than simulacra? Didn't seem right.

Chaz squeezed him on the shoulder. "It's better this way. He'll be able to enjoy what's left of his life, you know?" He dug in his pocket, then dropped a handful of change onto the windowsill. "Here. From the burrito stand."

Chaz wandered off to dig out an India Pale Ale. Davis stewed, then checked his mission parameters. Again. Two cases today. The one out on the street corner, then another near Warsaw Street at 20:17. Deviation percentage might be high by then, particularly if Chaz was in a mood today, but they could still do some good. Help cases going on in the real world. Get information to the real cops.

And Warsaw Street. 20:17.

Davis finally took the handful of coins and began sifting through them, holding each up to the morning sunlight coming through the window, checking the date. Chaz sauntered back over, then shook his head at Davis. "We could go to a bank, you know. Ask them for an entire *bucket* of coins."

"Wouldn't count," Davis said, frowning at the quarter he was holding. Did he have 2002, Philadelphia mint? He pulled out his phone, scrolling down.

"Wouldn't count?" Chaz asked. "By whose rules?"

"My own rules."

"Then change them."

"Can't," Davis said. Yeah, he'd found a 2002 already. It was

2003 he needed. Hard to find a place that used coins these days. The street vendors, the occasional convenience store.

"You do realize," Chaz said, "how much more difficult you make your life, don't you?"

"Sometimes," Davis admitted. "But I can't cheat, or the collection will lose all meaning. Besides, Hal knows the rules." Davis had gotten an email from his son last week; the kid had almost finished a complete set of the 2000s. There was a soda machine in Hal's school that gave real-money change.

"Let's say you find one in here," Chaz said. "Some little bit of metal that happens to have the right stamp on it, to make you all freaked out or whatever. What would you do? We can't take anything out of the Snapshot."

"Unless it's inside us," Davis said, nodding to Chaz's beer.

"You'd—"

"Eat the coin? Sure. Why not? What are the precinct bean counters going to do? Search my stool?"

Chaz took a long drink of beer. "You're a strange little dude, Davis."

"You're only now figuring this out?"

"I'm slow," Chaz said. "And you, you're like subtly weird, Davis. *Stealth* weird."

Davis's watch buzzed, and he checked the time. Five minutes. He leaned in, watching the building across the street. A bar with some apartments on top.

Chaz reached for the holster under his arm.

"You won't need that," Davis said.

"A man can dream, can't he?" But he did let go of the gun. "What makes this guy special anyway? A thousand murders a year in the city, and this one gets a Snapshot?"

Davis didn't answer. Seriously, couldn't Chaz be bothered to check the news once in a while? Or *at least* read the case notes?

They barely heard the shot across the street. Standing where they were, the little pop could have been almost anything. Someone flinging a bottle at a dumpster, a window breaking, even a door slamming. Davis jumped anyway.

Their perp, Enrique Estevez, hurried out of the building's stairwell a minute later, hands shoved in his pockets. He looked around nervously, then set off down the street. Not quite at a run, but still obviously agitated.

"I'm off," Chaz said.

"Don't let him see you."

Chaz gave him the look that meant, *What, you think it's my first day?* Then he was out the door tailing Estevez, phone in hand.

Davis ducked out a moment later and turned down an alley, following the map on his phone toward Sixth. He would wait at the last point Estevez had been seen on the real day, in case Chaz lost the trail.

Davis called Chaz on the phone. "How's he looking?"

"Nervous," Chaz said over the line. "Street's gone empty. Only a handful of people here. Should I take pictures of anyone, so the IRL cops can seek out witnesses?"

"No," Davis said. "Too suspicious. And what would they witness? That Estevez was on the street? Just tail him."

"Right," Chaz said. "Hold up. He turned toward Eighth."

Davis stopped in place. It was the wrong direction. "You sure?"

"Yeah. Is this a problem?"

"He was seen on Sixth in a few minutes," Davis said. "Is he turning back?"

"No, we're heading east, crossing avenues. Seems determined now. Not looking around as much."

Davis cursed quietly, turning on his heels and heading back along the alleyway at a swift pace. The eyewitness who claimed to have seen Estevez on Sixth was wrong—either that or a Deviation had sent their subject in the wrong direction. If the percentage was that high already, this entire Snapshot would be a wash.

"I'm moving parallel to you," Davis said, trying to keep himself from getting nervous. "You at Eighth yet?"

"Just passed it," Chaz said. "Damn, Davis. He ducked into an alleyway, heading south. It's going to be really hard to follow without looking suspicious."

They couldn't risk that. If Estevez got suspicious, it could create a ton of Deviations in his behavior. That was one type of Deviation they *could* do something about.

"I'm to the south on Twenty-First now," Davis said. "I'll bet I can intercept him."

He stopped on the corner at Eighth Avenue, trying to hide the fact that he was puffing from the short jog. He'd have never passed fitness requirements for IRL fieldwork. Not anymore.

Still, he'd gotten into position fast enough to catch sight of Estevez leaving an alleyway ahead. Estevez turned east along Twenty-First Street, and Davis followed.

"I've got him," Davis said, strolling along, trying to look nonchalant. Just another guy talking on his phone. Nothing to notice or worry about.

Damn. He was already feeling nervous. Stupid. This was a simple chase. He could do this without becoming a wreck.

"Nice work," Chaz said. "I'm heading east on Twenty-Second, parallel to you."

"Roger."

Davis kept pace with Estevez. The perp was a thin man, but taller, more . . . intimidating than his mug shots had made him seem. He'd made a big mistake—not just in murdering a man, but in picking the man to murder. The mayor's nephew.

This was already ramping up to be a big case for the prosecutor, who felt he'd have heavy hitters in the city leaning on him. Unfortunately, their case against the accused wasn't strong. So he'd requested a warrant for a Snapshot.

The city government of New Clipperton had bought the Snapshot Project. Paid the Restored American Union through the nose for it. But what did they know about how it worked? Barely anything. One of those ... *things* was trapped somewhere, kept unconscious, electricity buzzing through it and doing this. Re-creating days, in their entirety, from provided raw matter.

Well, you had a small window to get a Snapshot of a specific day made. A few weeks, and that was it. You had to start it up in the morning, insert people right away. If you waited it grew more difficult. Like the doorway in just wouldn't open. And getting data out ... well, the cops had to carry it out with them. You could usually get secure texts through, but even with those there was interference sometimes.

Privacy watchdogs had lost their minds when they'd found out about the Snapshot Project. Particularly when they'd discovered that originally, the mayor had been using it for personal enjoyment, details redacted.

The resulting flurry of laws and restrictions meant that you needed a court order to re-create a day, and it could only be used for official government business. They could technically send in drones to record what was happening, and the precinct had experimented with that. Might eventually move to it full-time, but for now, old-fashioned detective work seemed most effective. This way you could put a cop on the stand to testify about what he'd seen with his own eyes. Juries responded to that sort of thing.

He was proud of how he stayed on Estevez's tail with no sign of alerting the man. Like a real cop.

Chaz met him at an intersection, and the two kept following as Estevez called someone on the phone. They were too far back to hear anything, but the end result was that they saw when the man knelt down at the edge of the sidewalk and fumbled with something, then stood and darted down another alleyway.

Chaz cursed, speeding up, but Davis caught him by the arm.

"He's getting away!" Chaz said, reaching under his arm for his gun again.

"Let him. This was what we've been waiting for."

"This?" Chaz asked.

Davis walked up to the place where Estevez had knelt: a storm drain on the side of the road. He peered down, then reached in with his phone and took a few pictures. He held it up, scrolling between them until he found a good shot.

A handgun lay in the filth of the drain. "Murder weapon," Davis said, standing up and showing Chaz. "The IRL detectives have been searching for this in all the wrong places." He attached it to a message, then opened the secure HQ communication app on his phone.

He sent the message to Maria, their HQ liaison. *Murder weapon found,* he wrote. *Storm drain in front of a beauty salon on the north side of Twenty-First, between Tenth and Eleventh Avenues.*

"I hate just letting him go," Chaz said, folding his arms.

"You hate not being able to get into some kind of gunfight," Davis said back.

He waited, worried he'd need to send the message again. You never could be certain what would get out. Fortunately, a few minutes later his watch buzzed, and he glanced at the phone. A line was open, for the time being.

Intel received, Maria sent. *Nice work. Between Tenth and Eleventh? That's far from where you should have been.*

Eyewitness is wrong, Davis sent back. *Estevez went east after the murder, not west.*

Chance of Deviation? Maria sent.

Ask the bean counters, Davis replied. *I'm just reporting what I've found.*

Roger. Sending a team to that gutter IRL. Stay close in case they need follow-up.

Davis showed the phone to Chaz.

"So . . ." Chaz said, looking around. "We have some time. You want to head to Ingred Street?"

"It's noon," Davis said dryly.

"And?"

"And it's a school day."

"Oh. Right. What, then?"

"Well, we had some million-dollar burritos," Davis said, nodding toward a diner. "Shall we have some million-dollar coffee to wash them down?"

Two

Davis couldn't help wondering how the people in the diner would react to knowing they were dupes. The fat lady behind the counter, going over receipts. The two white guys in flannel and trucker caps, chewing on Reubens and grunting at each other. The mom with a gaggle of kids, hushing them with force-fed fries.

Davis felt he could take the measure of a man or woman by the way they handled the news that they weren't real. It was uncomfortable, intimate, and fascinating to watch. Some got angry, some got morose. Others laughed. You saw something about a person in that moment that they wouldn't ever know—couldn't ever know—about themselves.

His watch buzzed as the waitress arrived with a plate of fries for him and topped off his coffee. Davis had momentary sadistic visions of himself guessing the reactions of the people in the room, then pulling out his badge and showing it around to see if he was right. Trouble was, Chaz might do something like that if he got too bored.

Chaz got back from the restroom as Davis was munching on fries. "Sure," Chaz said, sitting, "you'll put mustard on *those*."

"Mustard belongs on fries."

"Like it belongs on burritos."

"Disgusting."

"You just aren't willing to live, Davis," Chaz said, stealing a fry. "Try new things, you know?"

"Once again, this isn't new," Davis said, checking the message on his phone. "You literally have been trying to get me to eat like you for *three years*."

"It's why I'm a good detective," Chaz said. "Tenacity. What's hottie pants say?"

"Hottie pants? Maria?"

Chaz nodded.

"She's like twenty years older than you."

"And hot. What does she say?"

"They found the gun in real life," Davis said. "It was down there in the storm drain where Estevez threw it. Soaked in ten days' worth of grime, but they rushed it through ballistics and it came back a match for the bullet. We might have to testify." They now had enough evidence to convict Estevez, and the testimony of two hardworking cops would only reinforce that.

Chaz grunted. "Would still feel better if I'd been able to gun that punk down. Pay him back, you know?"

"You don't even know what he did," Davis said dryly.

"Killed someone. That . . . um . . . girl?" He shrugged. "Anyway, want to play hooky for the rest of the day?"

Davis looked up, feeling a cold jolt.

"Our next job," Chaz continued, stealing another fry, "it's not till . . . what, almost twenty-one hundred?"

"Quarter after twenty. Domestic disturbance. They want us to see who hit first. Corroborate one story or the other."

"What a waste of our time."

Davis shrugged. It wasn't uncommon to go on small missions like that throughout the day, after the main case had been investigated.

"I don't want to wait around eight hours to see who slapped who," Chaz said. "Let's save everyone some time and money and bug out of here. The shrink says I should let her know if I feel 'emotional distress.'"

"Which means what?"

"Hell if I know. She seems to think that I should find living in Snapshots distressing."

"Seriously?" Davis said. "You? Is she paying *any* attention?"

"She's not even hot," Chaz added.

Davis sighed, but it did little to cover his sudden anxiety. They couldn't leave. Could they?

Maybe that would be for the best. . . .

No. Warsaw. 20:17. He had an appointment.

"Come on," Chaz said. "Let's go. I'll even let you push the button to turn the Snapshot off."

"I *always* push the button," Davis said.

"And today I won't complain."

"No, look, I've got something for us to do." Davis scrambled to pull out his phone again. "I've been reading the scanner forums—"

"Not again."

"—and there was a blip about this day, when it happened for real. Though I couldn't find anything in the precinct records, the *forums* claim that multiple squad cars were called in to search an apartment building. That will happen in the Snapshot in about an hour. Want to get there first and see what it was?"

"Forums," Chaz said dryly. "*Conspiracy* forums. You said there wasn't anything in the official records."

"Nothing I was allowed to see."

"Which probably means they didn't find anything."

"No. That would have been logged. There was *nothing there.*"

"Which means you didn't have clearance. They didn't want low-level detectives knowing about it, whatever it was."

"And doesn't that make you curious?" Davis asked. "We

could do a little real detective work. Snoop. Who knows, maybe someone will try to shoot you."

"You think so?" Chaz asked, perking up.

"It could happen. You're very shootable."

He nodded. "Yeah. Real detective work, eh?" He rubbed his chin. "You know what we're going to find, right? Some politician with a whore. That's why they'd hide it. Assuming it's even real, and the forum nutjobs aren't making things up."

"Yeah, well, I suppose we could just play hooky," Davis said. "Go back to the boring real world. Sit around. Watch a movie. Instead of living in one . . ."

"All right, I'm sold," Chaz said, standing. "But I've got to go hit the head first."

"Again?"

"That burrito, man." He shook his head. "That burrito . . ." He wandered off in the direction of the bathroom.

Davis relaxed his fist and let himself breathe out, trembling. They'd stay in the Snapshot for now. Davis paid the bill with actual cash, but the diner only gave change as credit. That wouldn't ever reach him though. This Snapshot city existed on its own, without external infrastructure. If people left the area the Snapshot covered, they vanished immediately. If someone was scheduled to enter the city, the Snapshot created their body and vehicle, then set them on the road driving in at the proper time.

He'd never been able to figure out the details. How did credit transactions work for those inside here? How did the Snapshot manage to re-create all outgoing and incoming transmissions? The power lines. The internet. Sunlight. What were the levels of reality for it all? He ate food in here. How much would he have to eat before the system recognized him as part of it, rather than being real? If he had too many burritos, would that badge someday shine for him, as it did for the dupes?

He tore himself away from that line of thinking. *Keep focused on my task.* He turned around in his seat, looking toward the woman with the children as she packed them up and herded them out the door. The oldest was six, self-proclaimed to his sister in an argument.

That was two years younger than Hal, but Hal had always been small for his age. Like his dad.

The mother and her children left, and Davis found himself staring at a different woman, sitting close to the back of the diner near the window. Slender, with black hair cut short. Angular features. Pretty. Very pretty.

"Well," Chaz said, stomping up, "there's another part of me added to the system: my dump. It'll get recycled when the day breaks down, right?"

"I suppose," Davis said absently, still watching the woman.

"Good to know that part of me will get used the next time

they rebuild this. My dump will be recycled into lawyers. Cool, eh?"

"How is that any different from real life?"

"Well, it . . ." He trailed off, scratching his head. "Oh. Yeah, I suppose you're right. Huh. Well anyway, you going to go talk to her?"

"Who?"

"The hottie back there."

"What? *No.* I mean, you shouldn't say things like that."

"Come on," Chaz said, nudging him. "You're staring at her hard enough to throw sparks. Just go say hello."

"I don't want to harass her."

"Talking isn't harassing."

"I'm pretty sure it's one of the *primary* methods of harassment," Davis said.

"Yeah, maybe, sure. But she's looking back at you. She's interested, Davis. I can tell."

Davis toyed with the idea, a small panic rising in him like an exploding bomb. "No," he said, standing. "Why bother? It's not real anyway."

"All the more reason to give it a go. For practice."

Davis shook his head and led the way out of the diner. Unfortunately, as they passed the woman's table, Chaz stepped over to her. "Hey," he said. "My friend is kind of shy, but he was wondering if maybe he could have your number."

Davis felt his heart all but stop.

The woman blushed, then looked away.

"Sorry to bother you," Davis said, hauling his partner out the door by the arm. Then, once outside, he continued, "You idiot! I said not to do that."

"Technically," Chaz said, "you told me *you* weren't going to do it. You didn't say that I couldn't."

"That was humiliating. I—"

Davis froze as the door to the diner opened and the woman stepped out. She blushed again, then handed Davis a little slip of paper before ducking back into the restaurant.

Davis stared at it, reading the phone number scrawled across the front. Chaz grinned a big, goofy smile.

Sometimes, Chaz, he thought, tucking the paper away, *I love you.*

"So, where are we going?" Chaz asked.

"Fourth," Davis said, leading the way down the street.

"Bit of a hike."

"Autocab?"

"Nah," Chaz said, hands in pockets. "Just saying."

They strolled for a time, Davis feeling the paper in his pocket. He was shocked, even embarrassed, by how pleased he was. How warm it made him feel. Even if he was never going to call her, even if she wasn't real. Damn. He hadn't felt like this in years, since before meeting Molly.

"You ever wonder," Chaz said as they walked, "if we should be using this more?"

"What do you mean?"

Chaz nodded at the cars passing on the wide avenue. At least half were autocabs, smooth and careful, each one coordinated with the others. A variety of older cars joined them, and most were just as smooth—but you could tell the manual drivers from the way they jerked about, making a mess of things. Like fish that had suddenly split away from the rest of the school.

"We should use this more," Chaz repeated. "We're in a day that already happened. So shouldn't we be able to ... I don't know ... buy lottery tickets or something?"

"And win money that will vanish when the day ends?"

"We could swallow it," Chaz said. "Like you said."

"There's a big difference between one coin and millions in lottery earnings. Not that they pay out instantly anyway, for the types of winning numbers we could look up ahead of time. Besides, it would likely be classified as counterfeiting if you somehow *did* get money out."

"Yeah." He shoved his hands in his pockets. "It would still be fun to win. Anyway, I just feel we should be able to do more. Get right what someone else got wrong."

"Which is what we do."

"I'm not talking about legal stuff, Davis." He sighed. "I can't explain it."

The two crossed the road, and cars started again behind them. A few old combustion engines roared past, making Davis turn. That was a sound from his past. Like the smell of gasoline.

"I understand," he said.

"You do?"

"Yeah."

That seemed to comfort the taller man. "So, any idea what we're looking for when we arrive at this place of yours?"

"I don't know," Davis said. "It's just one of those blips that the forum people notice. Sudden, urgent call for a car, several responses . . . then silence. No report. No nothing."

"And you think someone's scared we'll find out."

They'd talked about this sort of thing before. In here, the two of them were absolute authorities. Flashing their badges could get them past any obstruction, overrule any order. They were two men in a crowd of shadows.

In here, they were the only ones with rights. In here, they were *gods*. The longer he'd been working in Snapshots, the more Davis had realized that there were certain people on the outside who found his power in here terrifying. They hated thinking that there were simulacra of them that a couple of low-level detectives could order around. How to contain them, protect people's privacy, was a constant argument.

"I'm surprised," Chaz said as they finally reached Fourth

Avenue, "that they didn't remember to send us to some saferoom."

Davis nodded. They wouldn't have gone—they never did. But the precinct continued to order it, claiming that if Davis or Chaz were to meet their own dupe selves in the city, they'd be mentally scarred. Which was stupid.

"If we don't find anything at this address of yours," Chaz said, "I'm going to take the day off."

"Fair enough. But I think there will be something. It's suspicious."

"I'm telling you. Politician with a whore."

"They wouldn't call in squad cars for that." He chewed on his lip. "Have you noticed how lately they seem to have us do only the least work possible on a case? Find a murder weapon, witness a criminal activity. No interviews, little *real* police work."

"Guess they decided they don't want us getting too comfortable with that sort of thing," Chaz said. "Hell, they don't want IRL detectives in here. That's why they send guys like us in the first place."

The site of the mysterious call for the authorities—a call that wouldn't come in the Snapshot for about another hour—was an old apartment building with tags and graffiti sprayed all over it. The broken and grimy windows proclaimed it wasn't occupied these days.

"Doesn't look like the kind of place *I'd* take a prostitute," Davis noted.

"Like you've ever taken a prostitute anywhere," Chaz said, shading his eyes and looking upward. "I know this area. It was nice once—these were probably expensive apartments."

They walked up the steps, then tried the door, which was locked tight. Davis looked to Chaz, who shrugged and kicked the door in. "Damn," he said. "That was easier than I thought it would be."

"Feel like a real cop?"

"Getting there," he said, then peeked into the hallway.

A quick search didn't turn up anything. The ground floor apartments were open, doors unlocked, but they had been gutted and were empty save for the nest some homeless person had made beneath more spray-painted tags. Even the nest seemed like it hadn't been used in months.

Something smelled off. Musty? Davis wandered back into the main stairwell—near the entry door—sniffing at the air.

Chaz started toward the stairs to the second floor. "There are like twenty stories in this place, Davis. If we have to search them all, so help me, you'll owe me a burrito. Extra mustard."

"Let's try down first," Davis said, catching Chaz and pulling him to a door in the lobby, cracked open with only darkness beyond. He pulled it fully open, revealing a stairway leading down. The smell was stronger. Musty dampness.

Chaz tried the light switch, but the building's power was off. Davis dug out a small flashlight and shined it down the stairs.

"Convenient," Chaz said, trying his phone, which wasn't as good at providing light.

"Always used to carry a flashlight," Davis said, starting down the steps. "IRL, as a detective. You'd be surprised at how often it came in handy."

At the bottom of the steps was another door, which Chaz opened with a well-placed kick. Dampness wafted over them as they stepped into the basement, which had walls lined with broken mirrors. Some old exercise weights lay abandoned in the corner.

"See," Chaz said, holding up his phone for light. "This place was fancy, once upon a time."

Davis led the way through the basement gym, darting his light right, then left, growing nervous. But there didn't seem to be anything down here. They might have to wait until the phone call was made—and the squad cars showed up—to find out what it was.

Chaz stayed close to him, directing his phone's frail light. Perhaps the call had come because one of the floors had caved in or something. Wouldn't that be fitting? Two washed-up detectives, killed in a fake world because they couldn't be bothered to sit back and take a break.

Chaz poked his side, then pointed. Davis turned his flashlight in that direction, noticing a doorway in the wall. Light reflected off a tiled floor beyond. And beyond that . . .

"Water?" he said, striding forward. The musty smell suddenly made sense. "Swimming pool? How is it still *full* in this place?"

"Damned if I know," Chaz said, walking with him into the room. It *was* a pool, moderately sized, considering it was in an apartment building basement. Davis put his hand on his hip, shining the light around. The pool was only partially full. There was no—

His flashlight passed over a face underneath the water.

Davis froze, holding the light on the dead, glassy eyes. Chaz cursed, fumbling for his gun, but Davis just stood there staring. She was young, maybe just a teen. Beside her was another body, settled on the bottom of the pool, facedown.

Shaking, Davis turned his flashlight more slowly across the bottom of the pool. Another. And another.

Corpses. Eight of them.

Three

What the hell, man?" Chaz said. "What the *hell*!"

Davis sat on the steps of the apartment across the street from the one where they'd found the bodies.

"I mean . . . *what the hell*." Chaz paced back and forth, handgun out. Davis couldn't blame him. He clutched his own gun before him, feeling as if some murderer were going to pop out from behind the building, wielding a rusty cleaver.

"How did they keep this quiet?" Chaz demanded. "There are *eight* bodies in that building. Eight! How is this not on every news station in the city, right? How come they don't have every cop in the city working on this? Damn it!"

He paced back the other direction.

I deserve this, Davis thought, slumped in his place. *I should have just left well enough alone.* All he'd wanted to do was keep Chaz in the Snapshot until 20:17. Now . . . this.

"Okay, Chaz," Chaz said to himself, walking back the

other way. "Okay, okay. They're not *real* corpses, you know? Just dupes. Dead dupes. That's all you saw." He looked to Davis. "Davis? You okay, buddy?"

Davis held his gun in a trembling hand.

"Davis?" Chaz said. "What do we do now, man? You're a real cop. What do we do?"

"I'm not a real cop," Davis said softly.

"Yeah, not anymore. But you were one for . . . ten years?"

"I was on the force for ten years," Davis said. "But I was never a real cop."

Chaz, on the other hand, had been on the force for less than a year before being assigned to Snapshot duty to replace Davis's old partner, who had finally retired.

"So, what do we do?" Chaz asked.

"Two options, I guess," Davis said, holstering his gun. He took a deep breath. "We walk away, assume the IRL detectives are working on this, and pretend we didn't see anything. We erase our phone tracks, claim we hung out in the diner a few hours longer, and forget this happened."

"Okay, yeah," Chaz said, nodding. "Yeah. No reason we *have* to be involved, right? And they obviously don't want us knowing about this. So if we walk away, nobody is the wiser." He looked down at the handgun he was holding. "What's the other option?"

"Well, we're stuck here until that domestic disturbance in

the evening. We can poke around at these murders, maybe find out a thing or two that can help with the investigation. And if not . . . well, maybe we can figure out why the hell the precinct is hiding this from us. Those corpses look kind of fresh—not much bloating, not a lot of flesh sloughing off. Eight bodies found drowned in an old apartment building, and not a peep to the guys who could go back in time and find out who did it? Why the hell wouldn't they involve us?"

"Yeah." Chaz looked to him. "Yeah, *damn*. What's going on?"

People became cops for a myriad of reasons. For some it was expected—it was a family thing, or just seen as good work for a blue-collar person. Others, they liked the power. Chaz was one of those.

But deep down, there was something in all of them. Something about wanting to *fix* the world. Whether you joined up because your family pushed you into it, or just because you got recruited at the right time, there was a story you told yourself. That you were doing something *good*, something *right*.

That story was hard to keep believing, some days. Other days it walked up, slapped you in the face, and said, "You going to do something about this or not?"

A good way to go out, Davis thought. *Doing something that feels real again.*

"You want to dig into this, don't you?" Chaz asked.

"Yeah," Davis said, standing. "You with me?"

"Sure. Why the hell not." Chaz shivered, then finally put his gun away. "What do we do?"

"We wait," Davis said, checking his phone.

A short time later, an autocab pulled up and a couple of people got out. White people, wearing business clothing. *Real estate agents,* Davis guessed. *Or maybe people from a bank that owns this place.* The woman dug in her purse for some keys while the man pointed at the broken windows, saying something Davis couldn't hear.

They seemed concerned by the forced door. Hopefully that wouldn't introduce too big a Deviation. They went inside, chatting.

They rushed back out a few minutes later, visibly agitated. The man sat down on the steps, hyperventilating, holding his face. He threw up a short time later. The woman screamed into her phone, hysterical.

It took about ten minutes for the squad cars to come. There were two, joined by a third later, which arrived about a minute earlier than Davis's records said they would, without lights on. Davis didn't recognize any of the cops, but since he'd been on Snapshot duty for years, that wasn't odd. He knew people back at the precinct headquarters, but not a lot of the beat cops.

Several cops consoled the real estate agents, while the others secured the building. Why wasn't there anything in the precinct records? A complete hush. According to the forums, the cars would be gone in under a half hour.

"This is so *weird*," Chaz said. "What the hell is going on?"

"No idea," Davis said softly. "But I think I know how we can find out."

Chaz looked at him, then smiled. He seemed to be coming to grips with what they'd seen. "HQ?"

Davis nodded.

Not the real one, of course. The fake one, inside the Snapshot.

"Let's go," Chaz said, growing eager. "It's been months since we had an excuse to do this."

Four

Davis and Chaz burst in through the front of the 42nd Precinct headquarters, which housed Snapshot detail, among other special jurisdictions in the city. Davis tried to project confidence like Chaz did. But it was hard. In the real world when he visited this place, he felt small. Out of place. Maybe even scorned.

He paused inside the doors. The smell of coffee, the bustling of officers, everyone doing what they should—and everyone seeming to know Davis's shame. That he'd failed them, and been banished as a consequence.

Fortunately, he had Chaz. "Insecurity" wasn't really part of that man's vocabulary. Chaz held his reality badge up high in the air and shouted, "Guess what, everyone. Y'all ain't real!"

He sauntered forward, holding the badge and pointing it one way, then the other, grinning like he'd just won the lottery. Most people who saw it, they stopped and got that glassy look. Gina Gutierrez dropped her cup of coffee, which sent a spray into the air as it struck the floor. Marco's jaw hung open, then he patted at his body as if trying to prove to himself that he was real.

Davis followed his partner, feeling an initial stab of pain for the officers who saw the badge. Then his empathy was consumed by memories of the last time he'd come into this room, in the real world. Gina had looked at him as if he were a rat slinking into the middle of a wedding feast. Marco had refused to speak to him.

People swarmed around tables, popping up from behind cubicles—each one wanting to see the badge for themselves. There was no reason for Chaz to display it as he did, held over his head for all to see. They could have been surgical, moved right to Maria's cubicle, showed her the badge and gotten information without making a fuss. That was the sort of thing they were supposed to do. Fewer Deviations.

Davis didn't chide his partner. Maybe those Deviations would stop Warsaw at 20:17 from happening, which was something a part of him really, really wanted.

Maria's cubicle was in the rear half of the large workroom. Chaz and Davis settled into the cubicle doorway, looking in at her as the sounds of whispers, even tears, began around them.

Maria was a prim woman in her early fifties, with glasses

and hair she kept dyed black. She looked at the two of them over her spectacles—a sign of her stubbornness, as she'd always refused surgery to rid her of them—and focused on the badge in Chaz's hand.

"How'd you fake that?" she asked, turning back to her cubicle wall, which had a few virtual screens hovering before it.

"No faking, Maria," Davis said, taking the spare seat in the cubicle. Chaz loomed overhead like a lighthouse beacon, badge in hand. "I'm afraid you're a dupe. We're in a Snapshot."

She grunted, but otherwise didn't seem bothered. She knew, despite what she'd said, that they weren't faking. Dupes always knew. But she always reacted this calmly, which was one reason she was who they came to for information. Some people were reliable even after finding out that nothing they did mattered in the slightest.

"There was a call," Davis said, ignoring Holly Martinez as she stepped up, pulled Chaz around to get a look at the badge, then stumbled back, hand over her mouth. "About an hour ago now, to an apartment complex over on Fourth. For some reason, it isn't logged into my database when I check precinct call records."

"That means you aren't authorized to see the case," Maria said dryly. "You know the database is dynamic, based on clearance."

"I'm supposed to have full clearance."

"You do. There are just levels beyond 'full clearance.'"

"Well, fortunately, in here I have all those levels too." Davis reached up and tapped the badge that Chaz was holding.

Maria looked at it, momentarily transfixed. What *did* they see?

"I'll have to check with the chief," she said, tearing her eyes away from the badge.

"Check what?" Davis asked. "In here, I have ultimate authority. What happened at that apartment on Fourth?"

"Let me call the chief."

"No need," Chaz said, pointing as Chief Roberts barreled down the aisle between cubicles. He wore a suit; probably had meetings with politicians today. He never looked right in a suit, no matter how well it was tailored—they always ended up too tight on him.

He stormed right up to Chaz and took the badge from his fingers. The chief stared at it, then shoved it back at Chaz and barreled away without a word.

"Chief?" Maria said, standing up.

"Wait for it. . . ." Chaz said.

Davis sat back. He hated this part. He heard the door to the chief's office slam at the rear of the room.

The gunshot came a second later. Maria gasped, stumbling back against her desk, eyes widening.

"Looks like you're on your own," Chaz noted. "Feel free to go check if he's really dead. You do it about half the time."

She looked at him, her mouth moving silently. Then she sank down into her seat.

"How often?" she whispered. "How often do you do this?"

"Every six months or so," Davis said. "It's easier than trying to get information from you people IRL."

"I . . ." She took a deep breath. "What was it you wanted to know?"

"The call about an hour ago?" Davis prodded, speaking gently. "To Fourth Avenue? I think it was from some realtors."

Maria called up another screen, which popped into existence hovering above her desk. She tapped her fingers on the desktop, typing on an invisible keyboard. "Oh," she said. "*Oh* . . ."

"What?" Chaz said, leaning down beside Davis, both of them reading the screen. Information was coming in directly from the police investigating the old apartment building. Eight bodies. All presumed dead by drowning.

Fits previous pattern, one note said.

"Previous pattern?" Davis demanded. He reached over and tapped on her desk, calling up information. Pictures floated into the air—dead bodies with blue lips. Three people found suffocated, washed up on the shores of the city, in bags. They'd been preserved after death using chemicals.

The second discovery had been five bodies, this time found floating off the coast. They'd been in plastic bags, much like the first, though this time the deaths hadn't been from suffocation. Instead the victims had been poisoned.

"Daaamn," Chaz whispered.

"What connects these two sets to the corpses the group just discovered?" Davis asked, frowning and dragging some of the holo-pictures through the air above the desk.

"Looks like embalming fluid," Maria said, reading. "Discovered by detectives on the scene—which is important."

"It means finding these eight today was a lucky accident," Davis whispered, narrowing his eyes. "The others were dumped in the ocean, but these were found while the killer was still preparing them. Soaking them first, before dropping them off. So this is a chance to crack the case."

A quick scan of the files showed that detectives had been spinning their wheels until now. They were facing a meticulous killer who chose victims easy to miss: the homeless, prostitutes. It was sometimes shocking how the right people could vanish without anyone noticing—at least, not anyone who could make the cops or politicians pay attention.

He's clever, Davis thought, feeling a chill as he read the notes on those cases. *He's very clever. In fact* . . . Something struck him about it all, something that made him feel sick deep inside.

"This is Gina's case," Maria said. "She's leading, at least. We've got a ton of people on it. I've been following it too, for obvious reasons."

"Obvious?" Chaz asked, reaching across Davis and helping himself to some M&M's on Maria's desk.

Maria frowned, then zoomed one of the windows, showing a report Gutierrez had written, dubbing the murderer "The Photographer."

"What?" Chaz asked. "Why that name? Does it have something to do with Snapshots?"

"He's killing them in a specific way," Davis whispered. "To prevent Snapshot detectives from being able to find him."

Maria nodded grimly. "The Photographer preserves the bodies after killing them, which prevents forensics from getting a specific bead on when they were killed. Then, he or she dumps the corpses in the ocean, letting them drift and eventually wash up. The killer obviously doesn't mind if they're found, might even want it, but is stopping us from using a Snapshot on the case. He or she knows that we'd need to be able to point to a specific day or place to get a warrant."

She scanned the report from today, which was still being updated by police on the scene.

Bodies show evidence of what we assumed earlier, one of them wrote. *Killer was letting them soak in the pool to make it more difficult to tell when they were dumped in the ocean.*

Davis nodded. "So why keep this quiet? Why hush the call today so soundly?"

"Best way to catch someone is to not let them know they're being chased." Maria grimaced. "This will blow up soon enough. We might as well keep this out of the news as long as possible though, right?"

There's more to it than that, Davis thought, scrolling through a window, scouring notes and reports. *Dangerous,* one of them read. *If people lose faith in Snapshots, the tool could be undermined in court.*

"You still should have told us," Davis said.

"Why?" Maria said. "What would be the point?"

"When we're in Snapshots of certain days," Chaz said, crunching on M&M's, "we could go poke at things. Get more information."

"Where?" Maria said. "When? Didn't you hear that the killer is *specifically* working to make you two irrelevant?"

Davis glanced at his partner. Maria was being too defensive. She often got this way, as did the others. He and Chaz, they weren't supposed to poke into the business of *real* detectives. To the rest of the department they were errand boys, sent to retrieve specific data and nothing else.

But the truth was, nobody seemed to know what to do with the Snapshots. The city had been pressured into buying the program, and so had sunk a ton of money into it—but privacy laws had then tied their hands tightly. It was a wonder that even two detectives were allowed in. And if the general public knew how much leeway Chaz and Davis took with their job . . .

Well, either way, it was a tool that—even years into the program—nobody understood, let alone knew how to properly exploit. But that still didn't explain why they'd hide so much from the cops working in them.

"What aren't you telling me, Maria?" Davis whispered.

She met his eyes defiantly. Then those eyes darted to the side as Chaz lifted his gun to her temple.

"Chaz," Davis said, sighing. "Don't kill her again, please."

"*Again?*" Maria demanded.

"Just talk to me, Maria," Davis said. "We usually don't kill you. I promise."

"It's a Snapshot, Maria," Chaz said. He shrugged. "Nothing we do in here matters. Tell the nice man what it is he wants to know."

"I don't know why they didn't tell you," she said, stubborn. "No, they didn't tell you about the case. No, they didn't want to use you to investigate it. I don't know why."

"You're lying," Davis said.

"Prove it."

Davis looked to Chaz, sighing.

Chaz shot her.

Bodies don't *jerk* as much as people think they do, even when shot in the head. They just kind of slump, like Maria did. A little puff from the gun blowing her hair, head bobbing as if tapped, and then . . . her body drooped in her chair. There wasn't even much blood—the bullet didn't exit the other side of her head. Some blood did come out her nose, and out the hole in her temple.

Chaz calmly held aloft his badge for the few people who were still there, those who hadn't wandered out at seeing the badge originally—or who hadn't been scared away by what the chief had done.

"You bastard!" Davis said, standing and stumbling back from the cubicle. "You actually did it!"

"Yeah," Chaz said. "I've always wanted to, you know? That smug look on her face. Treating us like she's a babysitter and we're a pair of three-year-olds."

"You *actually did it*!"

"What? You implied we'd done it loads."

"That was an interrogation technique!"

"A piss-poor one, judging by results," Chaz said, shoving her body off the chair and sitting down. "You going to help me look through this stuff? She's got better access than us. We might be able to learn something."

Davis spun about, scanning the precinct office over the cubicle walls. A few had remained at their stations, despite everything that had happened so far. Those had stood up at the shot, and now backed away from him. Friends . . . well, acquaintances. The fear in their eyes dug into him—like he was a terrorist.

Officer Dobbs had his gun out, and he looked at it, weighing it. Davis could almost read the conflict. *If I shoot him,* Dobbs seemed to be thinking, *I'm shooting a real person. A cop who didn't do anything illegal. But if I'm not real . . . who cares, right? I can't be punished, not really.*

Dobbs met his eyes, and Davis had the sudden instinctive feeling that he should draw his own sidearm and gun Dobbs down before the man could make the decision. But, frozen, Davis couldn't bring himself to do it.

Dobbs proved to be a better person, even as a dupe, than Chaz was. Dobbs holstered his weapon and shook his head, then stumbled away.

Davis breathed out a long sigh. Not relief, exactly. More weariness. He ducked down beside his partner, trying to ignore Maria's body bleeding on the floor.

Chaz wasn't looking at the case with the serial killer. He'd pushed all those windows to the side, and was instead looking up something else. Personnel files.

His own.

"Damn," Chaz said. "We should have done this ages ago, Davis. You see? She has full access to our records."

Chaz had only been in the New Clipperton force for a year before being assigned to Snapshots. Before that, he'd served in Mexico City, with which they had an immigration treaty and transferable citizenship. His Mexico City record commended him for eagerness and enthusiasm in training, though it also contained this line at the end: *Overly aggressive.*

"Aggressive," Chaz snapped. "What does that even mean? Rodriguez, you bastard. I mean, shouldn't a cop be aggressive? You know, in pursuing justice and the like?"

The rest of the record, which Chaz scrolled down, had notes from New Clipperton officers.

Eager. Strong willed. I think he'll cut it, Diaz had written before retiring.

Is a bully, Maria herself had written a few months into Chaz's tenure in the city, when he'd been a traffic cop. *I have seven complaints on this guy already.*

Treats being a cop like playing a video game. That from his former partner.

It was followed by another note from Maria. *Recommended for Snapshot duty. We can't fire him, not without a concrete incident. At least in there, when he inevitably shoots someone, it won't be grounds for a lawsuit.*

Davis glanced at her corpse again.

"Huh," Chaz said. "You read that?"

"Yeah."

"Diaz," Chaz said, raising his chin. "Hell of a guy, that man was. Strong willed? Yeah. Yeah, I'm strong. And I *could* have cut it, you know? If she hadn't stuffed me in here."

"Sure."

"Let's see what yours says," Chaz said, sliding his fingers across the desk to start the search.

Davis tapped the desk, freezing the windows. "Let's not."

"Come on. Don't you want to see?"

"I can guess," Davis said. "Bring those other windows back, the ones with the case notes about the Photographer. Load them to my phone."

Chaz sighed. "It would only be fair to read your record, Davis. You know why I'm here. What about you?"

"Aggression," Davis said.

Chaz looked at him, then laughed. Though it was technically true; aggression *was* his problem. Not enough of it.

They got the files loaded, then Davis tugged Chaz's shoulder, nodding for them to leave. "Let's get out of here before someone decides that being a dupe means they can gun us down with no consequences."

Chaz didn't argue. He slipped out, almost tripping over Maria's legs. Davis gave her one last glance, then—because he couldn't help himself—he grabbed her little change bowl from the desk and dumped the coins into his hand.

Together, the two of them left the precinct. Davis felt better standing out on the steps, under the sunlight—even though it was as fake as everything else here.

"What now?" Chaz asked.

Davis checked his phone. 14:07. He had six hours left. "I'm going to stop a monster. You with me?"

"Of course. I can cut it, Davis. I'm telling you, I *can*. This is our chance, you know. To prove ourselves. But where do we go?"

"Back to the apartment building with the corpses," Davis said, calling an autocab with a tap on his phone.

"To get information from the cops there?"

"No, I've got their report," Davis said. "We're going to talk to the people who own the building."

"The bank?"

"No," Davis said. "The *real* owners."

Five

avis spent the ride sorting through the coins that had been on Maria's desk, absently raising each one to the sunlight shining through the cab's window and checking the date it had been minted. American money; most city-states had adopted it, though the one- and two-dollar coins had both originally been Canadian.

It felt relaxing to study something like coins that was basically an anachronism. You could know everything there really was to know—now that no new ones were being made. Funny, how quickly they'd started to vanish. It had only been two years since the last coins had been minted.

Still, the story was finished. You could have all of the answers.

Wait, he thought, stopping on a nickel. He scanned through the list on his phone. 2001, Denver mint? He felt a little jolt of excitement. They'd both been missing the 2001 nickel. With this, he completed a set.

"What did you do, Davis?" Chaz asked. "Everyone else seems to know what landed you in here, but nobody will ever tell me. Did you shoot a kid?"

Davis ignored him, pocketing the coin, stupidly excited.

"I still don't get why you like those coins so much. They're old now, meaningless. Practically worthless."

"That's what my wife always said."

"Your *ex*-wife, Davis."

"That's what I meant."

He sifted through the rest of the coins, but didn't find any of interest. Unfortunately, they reminded him of Maria, lying on the floor of the precinct office. Her dead eyes staring at the sky, the neat little hole in her temple leaking blood.

He dug out his phone and, just to reassure himself, texted the real Maria outside the Snapshot.

Hey, he said. *Have you guys managed to catch the serial killer IRL? The one they call the Photographer?*

There was a long pause where no reply came. Finally, the message bounced, and—annoyed—he sent it again. This time it went through. Then a direct line opened to IRL.

How do you know about that, Davis? Maria sent as soon as it opened. He could sense the sharpness of her tone.

Your dupe told us, Davis wrote. *She considers it important, for some reason. I don't know. Said maybe we should poke into things while we wait.*

You aren't authorized for that case, IRL Maria sent. *If my dupe is talking about it to you, it means you've created a Deviation in her. Go to a saferoom. You're supposed to be there anyway. Are you ignoring protocol again?*

We're on our way now, Davis sent. *But did you catch him? The swimming pool corpses in the abandoned apartment building, they helped you track him down?*

Pause.

No, Maria admitted. *Those corpses haven't led to anything so far. Really, there's nothing you can do.*

He believed her, at least on the facts about the corpses. Maria didn't lie. She withheld information all the time, but would just stare at you if you tried to pry something out of her. She'd never lied to him about anything important.

That was far more than he could say about some people.

He showed the screen to Chaz, who nodded. "You ever wonder if the thing that powers this whole operation can see what we're doing?"

"I think it's supposed to be unconscious," Davis said, pocketing the phone. "It dreams up a re-creation of the day, and we slip in."

"So we're in its dreams." Chaz shifted, uncomfortable. "We pretend this is all technological, like we're in some simulation. But . . . I mean . . ."

"Close enough," Davis said. "Powered down with a button, powered on with some computer code. What's the difference?"

"Feels different. When I think about it. Maybe the thing is watching us."

"Maybe. But I don't think so. The way this all plays out . . . it doesn't feel like anything is watching. Otherwise, why the Deviations? Feels like the code instructs the thing to create an exact representation of the day, then just lets it play out naturally."

So far as they could tell, Snapshots proceeded exactly as the original day had, so long as nothing interfered. But that was hard to prove, as they couldn't monitor it. It had been tried before—they had let it run all day on its own, then checked at the end of the day by sending some drones in to look things over. But even that was suspect, as entering or leaving the Snapshot at any time except when it was just created tended to cause huge Deviations.

The best they could do was send two cops into the system, live it through and try to muddle along, hoping they didn't accidentally send the Snapshot running in the wrong direction. Of course, that plan didn't take into account the two of them shooting anyone or sending scores of people into chaos.

Davis sighed as the autocab pulled to a stop. He'd chosen a place a block or two from the run-down apartment building. He climbed out, taking a bottle of water from the cab's mini fridge—his account would be charged, but it was a fake version of his account. Outside the cab, he fished in his pocket for the nickel. His fingers touched crumpled paper—the woman's number, from the diner. He pulled out both, then shook his head and stuffed the paper back in his pocket.

"What's that?" Chaz asked.

"I found a nickel I don't have IRL," Davis said, washing off the nickel. Then he tried to swallow it. That wasn't as easy to do as he'd thought. He ended up on hands and knees, coughing the nickel onto the sidewalk, where it rested defiantly on the pavement.

"Damn," Chaz said. "Never thought you'd actually try that."

"Maybe," Davis said, swallowing a gulp of water, "I'll just ask the IRL Maria if I can trade for the one in her coin jar."

"Yeah," Chaz said, sounding amused. "Might be easier." He paused. "You're a weird little dude, Davis."

Once Davis had recovered himself, Chaz started off

toward the apartment building. Davis took him by the arm, shook his head, and pointed the other direction.

His search took some time—the cops showing up had scared off his targets. Still, after fifteen minutes he spotted a likely candidate: a kid standing on a street corner with hands shoved in the pockets of his longball jersey. He was wearing a ball cap and combat boots, the latest irrational fashion choice of kids on the street.

Davis wagged his phone at the kid, who nodded almost imperceptibly. Davis jogged over, Chaz following, curious.

"How much?" the kid said.

"Ten hits?" Davis said. "Stiff."

"I got five," the kid said, sizing him up.

Davis nodded. "You a Primero?"

"What's it to you?" the kid asked, getting the drugs from his pocket.

Davis stepped backward, raising his hands. "Look, I know what the Primeros do to people who sell on their turf. I'll find someone else."

"Settle your boots," the kid said. "I'm Primero." He flashed the proper sign. "Damn chippers. You shouldn't care who you buy from."

"I just don't want to get into trouble," Davis said, tapping his phone against the kid's, holding his thumb over the authenticator and transferring fake money for fake drugs to a fake person. "There's an apartment building three streets over," Davis added. "Old beat-up place. Has Primero tags sprayed all over it. Who've you guys been renting it to?"

The kid froze, five large white pills clutched in his hand.

"You cleared out the homeless people living there," Davis said. "Let someone else in. Kept everyone else away for him, right? Who is he?"

"You're a cop?" the kid said.

Davis took the pills, then popped one in his mouth and washed it down. "Would a cop do that?"

The kid stepped backward, then frowned.

"This guy," Davis said. "He's trouble. Big trouble. You don't need to know why we're hunting him, but I'm willing to buy information. Go tell your narco what I've said. I'll wait here for you to come back with him. He'll want to talk to us."

The kid bolted, and Davis looked back at Chaz.

"Damn," Chaz said softly. "Did you just take a full hit of stiff?"

In response, Davis popped the pill from his cheek and spat it out. He dropped all five pills and ground them beneath his shoe. He then took a long pull on his water bottle, hoping that he hadn't gotten too much of the stimulant into his system.

Chaz laughed. "So, you think the gang will actually come talk to us? I think that kid will just bolt."

"Maybe," Davis said, then settled down on a bench near the corner to wait.

It didn't take long. Six of them came together: the kid they'd been speaking to, four older teens, and one man in his thirties. That would be the narco—the head drug dealer for this little area. Not the head of the gang, but leader to a couple dozen kids on the street here. Half boss, half parent.

Davis stood and held his hands to the sides in a non-threatening way, and smothered his nervousness. The narco was a tall man, lighter skinned than Chaz or Davis, with buzzed hair. Davis could almost imagine him wearing a polo shirt and slacks on business-casual day at the office, rather than jeans and combat boots.

Davis and Chaz followed the group into an alleyway, and the narco pointed. Two of his men hopped up to Davis and Chaz, probably to search them.

"I've got a gun in my right pocket," Davis said. "My friend has one in the under-arm holster beneath his jacket. We'll want them back. Don't touch our wallets, or there will be trouble."

The gang members took the guns, to Chaz's obvious annoyance, then searched them for other weapons. But they left the wallets alone. Davis suffered it, eyes closed, trying to calm himself. Finally, the two cops were allowed to approach farther down the alleyway, which smelled of trash and stagnant water. Chaz looked back toward the street longingly and patted at his holster, already missing his gun.

"We should talk in private," Davis said to the narco.

"Why?" he demanded.

"Because you won't want what we tell you to spread," Davis said, meeting his eyes, trying to project a confidence he didn't feel.

The narco weighed him. An autocab passed on the street behind them with a quiet hum. Finally the narco nodded, and led the two of them farther into the alley. The rest of the gang members stayed put, one sighting on Davis with his own gun, as if in warning.

"You scared Pepe really well," the narco said. "He thinks you're feds. It was a cute trick, palming a hit of stiff in front of him. Tell me why I shouldn't just have you shot."

"If we were feds," Chaz noted, "you think that offing us would somehow be a *good* idea?"

Davis calmly reached to his pocket and took out his wallet, then opened it, revealing his reality badge.

The narco's eyes caught on it. They widened, mesmerized, almost like he had taken a hit of some drug. He whispered a soft prayer, then reached out with reverent fingers, touching the badge.

"You . . ." The narco swallowed. "You said you weren't cops."

"I never said that," Davis said, not putting the badge away. "I said we were willing to pay for some information. About the person renting a specific apartment building from you."

"You've gotten yourself into something bad, friend," Chaz said. He pulled out a cigarette and put it in his mouth, but didn't light it. He'd been trying to stop. "This guy who has been paying you? He's been murdering people. Prostitutes. Children. Anyone he can find who won't make waves."

The narco cursed softly.

Davis raised his phone, set to display his entire savings. A number larger than most cops would have been able to save. But he didn't have many expenses—just child support, really. He slept in a saferoom provided by the precinct, on the outskirts of the city, so he was less likely to run into himself while in a Snapshot.

"Tell us about this guy renting the apartment building," Davis said. "You knew there was something off about him, didn't you? Wipe that conscience clean, and you can take every penny of this. My payment to you."

"It's fake, isn't it?" the narco said, running his hand across his buzzed scalp. He swore something fierce. "It's all fake."

"Sure, sure," Davis said. "Completely fake. But you're the only one who knows it, friend."

"Take the money," Chaz suggested, leaning one shoulder against the wall. "Live it up for a day. They'll turn this Snapshot off sometime in the evening. You're going to vanish then. Might as well enjoy the time you have left."

Davis dangled the phone. The narco looked at it, then sank down beside the wall of the alleyway.

And started crying.

Chaz rolled his eyes. Davis looked at the street thug and felt a wrenching inside of him. Something about the Snapshot really must have made dupes realize they weren't real, once they saw the badge. The bean counters outside denied it, but they didn't live in here. Didn't see men like this, hardened criminals, crack and turn into children before the inevitable truth that their entire world was doomed.

Davis sank down and sat next to the man. He waved for Chaz to hand him the pack of cigarettes, then offered one to the narco.

"Mama always said those would kill me," the man said,

then laughed. Davis figured he'd been wrong about the narco's age. He wasn't in his thirties; he just looked older compared to the others.

The narco took a cigarette. Davis lit it up, then lit one for himself.

"I feel like the reaper sometimes," Davis said. "You know. Showing up, informing people that they're going to die in a few hours?"

The narco breathed in smoke, then exhaled it. He rested his head back against the wall, tears still streaming down his cheeks.

"What's your name?" Davis asked.

"Does it matter?"

"I'm real, kid," Davis said. "I'll remember your name."

"Horace," the kid said. "Name's Horace."

"Horace. You don't want the money, do you?"

Horace shook his head. "Won't make me forget, *ese*."

"Go home then. Hug your mom. But before you go, do some good. Tell me about this guy who has been renting that building from you."

"What does it matter?"

"He's killing kids," Davis said. "Sure, your life is over. That's tough. But hell, why not help us stop this monster before you go?"

Chaz shook his head, arms folded. In the mouth of the

alleyway, the other kids were whispering, looking panicked by the narco's actions.

"He's young," Horace whispered. "Maybe my age. Twenty-four, twenty-five. Asian. Quiet type. Creepy. We stay out of his business—figured he killed someone and wanted to hole up. But didn't think . . . you know . . ." He shuddered. "He won't come back. One of the kids spotted him running. Your people at his hidey-hole spooked him. He's gone."

"You have a name?" Davis asked. "Anything?"

"No name," Horace said, then took a puff of the cigarette. "You got some paper I can write on?"

Davis fished in his pocket and came out with a small piece of paper. The gangster took a pen from his pocket and wrote on it. An address.

"He wanted two places," he said softly. "With large tubs or pools in them he could fill. That's the second. A school, once. If he's smart, he'll run and you'll never see him. But people like him, they can be really smart in some ways but . . ."

"Really dumb in others," Davis said with a nod. "Thanks."

Horace shrugged, puffing on the cigarette. "You're right. I knew something was wrong about him. Watch out for yourself, *ese*. He's . . . well, I figured he was just crazy. But he knows."

"Knows?" Davis said, glancing at Chaz.

"That it isn't real," Horace said. "He kept saying it. This is a Snapshot; we're all part of a Snapshot. Got to get rid of the Deviations, he said. Warned me. Don't be a Deviation. . . ."

Davis felt a chill.

"Anyway," Horace said, "give me that cash." He held out his phone.

"You said you didn't want it."

"I don't." He pointed down the alleyway. "Those boys though, they're gonna get a bonus today. Spend a few hours in luxury. Don't tell them, okay?"

"I wouldn't dream of it," Davis said, tapping Horace's phone with his, transferring enough to buy a nice car.

Horace stood and stamped out the cigarette, leaving a little twist of smoke on the ground at Davis's feet as he walked down the alleyway. He adopted a stronger gait before he reached the kids. A practiced air of invincibility.

"Leave the guns!" Davis called to them, suddenly panicked by the thought of them running off with the weapons.

They dropped them in the mouth of the alleyway, then were gone.

"I can't believe that worked," Chaz said, arms folded. He looked at Davis. "How did you get him to talk like that?"

"He was scared," Davis said, forcing himself to his feet. "Guess I played off that."

"We never do stuff like this anymore," Chaz said. "Interview suspects. We can get them to talk when they never would IRL. We're really wasted in here, aren't we?"

"Maybe. Maybe not." Most of the testimony they could gather in here was inadmissible in court—if they found a witness, the IRL cops would have to get them to testify for real. And of course, a dupe's words couldn't be used against the real person in court.

It was all so sticky. Most cases involving Snapshots were arduous things, full of testimony on Deviations, possibilities, and technical arguments. The only thing that really held up was the testimony of the cops. They had to have good enough records to be viable witnesses, but also had to be officers the precinct wouldn't care about wasting in work that nobody else wanted to do.

The two of them collected their guns. "I didn't realize you'd started carrying," Chaz noted to him. "Least not until I saw that gun earlier."

"I've been doing it for a few months now," Davis said. The truth, as he'd wanted to get back in the habit. Though this was a new gun, his first time carrying it into a Snapshot.

He looked after the gang members, but couldn't spot them. They'd run off fast.

"Good thing this isn't real," Chaz said, shading his eyes from the late afternoon sun. "You'd be broke, friend. I had no idea you'd saved up such a nest egg. How'd you manage to do that?"

"Simple tastes," Davis said. And plans to buy a house someday. Him, his son, his wife . . .

Well, that was one dream that could die. "Come on," he said. "Let's check this second place out, though I'm worried. We've been racking up quite the list of Deviations. Try not to step on any butterflies on the way."

Chaz gave him a confused look, and Davis just shook his head, calling them another autocab.

Six

avis and Chaz stopped on the cracked sidewalk in front of a boxy monster of a building. It loomed, hollow, with windows too small to be comfortable. Like a prison. Which was, as Davis considered it, a very accurate comparison.

"Southeast High School," Chaz read from the sign—full of bullet holes—to their right.

"Closed two years ago," Davis said, reading from his phone.

"They were using that box up until two years ago?" Chaz said. "Damn. No wonder kids out here turn to selling drugs."

The school's front doors were wrapped in chains to keep them closed. Davis took a deep breath, and glanced at Chaz. Both took out their sidearms.

You could get killed inside a Snapshot, though it didn't happen as often as it did to cops IRL. You could anticipate your surroundings in the Snapshot, barring Deviations. You knew which thugs were likely to start shooting, and which situations were more dangerous.

Still, it happened. Most often it was something mundane. The woman Davis had replaced had died in a simple car accident. She'd insisted on driving a squad car instead of taking autocabs. She could just as easily have died on her way home from work, but she'd crashed here in the Snapshot.

It felt somehow wrong to think of a cop dying in the Snapshot. This place wasn't truly real. It shouldn't, therefore, have such real consequences. As Chaz always said, things you did in the Snapshot didn't really matter. . . .

"Locked tight," Chaz said, testing the chains on the front doors. Perhaps the killer had a key, but Davis suspected not. The front entrance was far too prominent; you couldn't sneak in bodies this way, even at night, without risking someone seeing you. So where?

He led the way across dead grass that hadn't been watered in years, sliding around the school to some kind of shipping entrance at the back, up a short ramp. Yeah, this was better. You could pull a car in here silently and unload.

He tried the door at the top of the ramp, and found it unlocked. He nodded to Chaz and both stepped inside, handguns pointed into the shadows.

"That's a nice gun," Chaz noted softly. "Taurus PT-92, right? Flashy. Pearl grip, even. Not what I'd have expected for you."

Davis didn't reply. Heart beating quickly, finger deliberately *not* on the trigger, he led the way through the echoing halls of the school. The debris here was somehow more *personal* than that back at the apartment building. Old discarded notebooks. Pencils with the tips broken off. A ball cap, a deflated soccer ball. This had been a lively place up until a few years ago.

That only made it feel creepier now. Haunted. Unlike the apartment building, which had been gutted, this place had been abandoned in haste. Nobody had wanted to be here—not students, administrators, or teachers.

They passed an old trophy case, the glass shattered, dust covering the plaques. Graffiti tags covered the walls. By now it was almost 16:00, and the sunlight sneaked into the place through boarded windows, reflecting off old tile floors and casting shadows. But it was enough for Davis to make out a sign on the wall without needing his flashlight. He waved his gun toward it, then pointed. Looked like the school had its own pool. An indoor one, near the gym.

Davis found himself sweating as they crept along the corridor. He jumped as a feral cat scurried out of one hall and down another one, into darkness. He was so startled, he nearly unloaded his gun at the thing.

You're going to have to confront this, he thought, heart racing as they moved inevitably forward. It had been years since he'd been in a position like this, but the memories came back, sharp like broken glass. A dark building. Calls for backup, and . . .

And Davis, useless.

Is this why you insisted on watching for cases like this? So you could prove to yourself you could do it? That you could pull the trigger?

He still let Chaz go first when they reached the pool. He stood outside the door—breathing hard, wiping his brow with a trembling hand—before finally forcing himself in through the door behind his partner. He'd waited too long, he knew. If there had been danger inside, Chaz would have been in trouble, alone.

There was no danger. There wasn't anything. They needed the flashlights again, but the pool was empty—not even any water. *Air feels humid,* Davis thought, forcing his breathing back under control.

"Huh," Chaz said, hands on hips. "Were we wrong?"

Davis waited until his trembling subsided, though he couldn't completely banish his tension—the pressure on his chest that made him feel like running away as fast as he could go. He pointed his light toward the locker rooms, then started that way. He peeked inside and found a table had been pulled in there, set with some cups and fast-food wrappers. Seemed newer than the rest of the school's debris.

"Careful," Davis said. "Someone *has* been here." He stopped in the doorway into the locker rooms until Chaz nudged him from behind; then he forced himself farther in, gun in one hand, flashlight in the other.

There was a place for demeaning group showers, and here someone had worked with a board and some caulk to turn it into a kind of tub. Yeah, this was the killer's hideout. He was preparing to soak some more bodies. The improvised tub was full of water, maybe four feet high, but there weren't any bodies in it yet. Perhaps the Photographer was seeing if his handiwork would hold.

We might be in time, then! Davis thought. *He might not have killed the next group.*

He immediately felt stupid. This was a Snapshot of life from ten days ago. Still, surely they could do *some* good, help catch the one doing this.

"Hey," Chaz said. "Check this."

Davis turned away from the showers, to where Chaz was shining his phone's light on a door that was shut tight, with a chair wedged under it and some rope tying the knob to a post beside the wall.

Davis hastened over, his tension rising again. That looked like an improvised lock to keep someone in. He nodded, and Chaz unwedged the door, then untied the rope. No sounds came from within. They shared a look, and then Davis let Chaz ease open the door, gun pointed downward so as to not accidently shoot any captives. It smelled foul inside, and Davis gagged.

"Bodies," Chaz said with a grunt, using his phone for light. "Damn, it smells terrible in here." He stepped forward.

His shoe *crunched*.

Chaz jumped backward, then the two leaned down. The floor in here was littered with insect carcasses.

Bees, Davis thought as Chaz opened the door farther. His flashlight highlighted the slumped corpses of people on the floor, surrounded by dead insects. The stench was overwhelming, and Davis had to breathe through his mouth.

Why bees? Davis thought as he inched into the room, brushing the insect carcasses from in front of him. There were hundreds, maybe thousands, of dead bees in here.

It started to make sense. His tension melted away before the academic facts, and he stood up in the dark room. It had been a storage room for old sports equipment. There were six people inside, all dead now.

"Check the corpses," he told Chaz. "See if they share

anything obvious. Age, gender." He barely noticed whether Chaz went to do it. Instead, he tucked away his gun and called up autopsy reports from the earlier murders.

He kept saying it. Horace the drug dealer's voice echoed in his memory. *This is a Snapshot; we're all part of a Snapshot. Got to get rid of the Deviations, he said.*

Don't be a Deviation.

The first group had died by asphyxiation. The cops assumed they'd been suffocated in the bags, but that didn't fit the pattern. They'd have been killed before being placed in the bags, right? The killer would have wanted to soak them first, to obscure how long they'd been in the ocean.

"Man," Chaz said. "These people look bad, Davis. Even for dead folk. I think I might need to throw up."

"Do it outside the room," Davis said absently.

There, he thought, pulling up the records of one of the bodies they'd identified. A prostitute. He scanned her medical records. Asthma. It was a connection. One of the others listed the same ailment. The others didn't list much, but they also didn't have any notes from next of kin. So maybe the information just hadn't been discovered.

The second group had died from poisoning. What was the theme? He scanned through the reports and happened across one note by an examiner. *All victims were extremely farsighted and wore corrective lenses.*

The third group—the bodies they'd found in the basement of the old apartment complex—clinched it for him. The officers there had left to find out why everyone was panicking back at the precinct office, but before abandoning their investigation they'd left a very important note.

These people all seem to have been naturally paralyzed.

"Ugh," Chaz said, walking back into the room, holding a bucket. "Davis? Damn it, man. Stop standing there in the middle of them. What's wrong with you?"

Davis looked around at the bodies. "You checked them all?"

"Mostly."

Davis tucked away his phone, then rolled over a body. Her face was covered in swollen bee stings—a horrible sight. He could see why Chaz had been disturbed.

"He's killing people he decides are Deviations," Davis said. "He thinks he's in a Snapshot."

"He *is* in a Snapshot."

"Yeah, but only his dupe is right," Davis said. "And it only does what the real him has already done. The killer thinks everything is a Snapshot, and he's trying to expunge the Deviations—which he sees as people who have some flaw in their biology. The first group had terrible asthma. The second group, bad vision."

Davis rolled over another corpse. "These people were allergic to bee stings. Look at these wounds—those aren't regular stings. He rounded up a bunch of people with terrible allergies, then locked them in here with bees. He's cleansing the city of Deviations."

"That doesn't make any sense."

Davis ignored him, inspecting the next victim, a woman who had died on her back with her eyes swollen shut. "Serial killers like this . . . lots of them are looking for power. *Control.* They feel they don't have control in their lives, so they control others. Imagine being paranoid. You get the idea you're in a Snapshot, that you're not real. How might you act?"

He looked up as Chaz shrugged. "Everyone's different," Chaz said. "You've seen it. Some wander off, some cry, some—"

"Some kill," Davis said.

"Yeah." Didn't happen often. Most people didn't have it in them to kill, even if they discovered something terrible like this. But once in a while, someone they showed a reality badge to immediately reached for a weapon, perhaps thinking—irrationally—if they killed the person with the badge, it would disprove what they'd just seen.

That was probably too simple for this killer. Davis looked back at the dead woman. This killer was already crazy; you had to be, to do something like this. But mix it with a belief that your world was a sham . . .

It was surreal. In here, the killer's dupe would be *right*. He *was* in a Snapshot. That didn't change the fact that out in the real world, there was someone killing entire groups of people. Real people. Not dupes.

The woman in front of him stirred.

Davis cried out, leaping backward, scrambling for his gun—though of course he wouldn't need it.

"What?" Chaz demanded.

"That one is still alive," Davis said, pointing, hand shaking.

The woman rolled her head over and whispered something. "Water?"

Davis knelt down. "Get some water," he said to Chaz. "Go!"

"Water," she whispered again.

"I'm getting some," Davis said. "We're cops. It's okay. Don't worry."

"He'll . . . come back. . . ." She couldn't open her eyes. They were swollen shut. She could barely move her lips.

"When?" Davis asked.

"Every night," she said. "Every night at seven thirty. He checks on us then. We were going to jump him . . . but . . ." She cursed softly. "It hurts. . . ."

Chaz returned with a cup from the desk outside, filled with water. He knelt down, but didn't move.

"Give it to her!" Davis said.

Chaz tried dribbling it onto her lips. She didn't move anything but her head, which she could barely rock. It seemed like some got into her mouth.

"Seven thirty," Davis said. "He'll be back at seven thirty?"

The woman whispered something, but even leaning down close, Davis couldn't make it out. Grimly, he checked the others. They were definitely dead.

The woman had started weeping. A tearless trembling.

Chaz stood up, then looked to Davis, who stared at the woman, horrified.

"I'll take care of this," Chaz said, getting out a pair of earplugs. "It's okay."

Davis nodded numbly, then forced himself to walk out.

A gunshot sounded behind him; then Chaz came to the doorway, his face ashen. Together they closed the door, put the rope back as they'd found it, and propped the chair in place. Chaz put the water cup back as Davis slumped down on a bench beside some lockers, licking his lips. His mouth had gone dry.

"So we wait here," Chaz said, "and catch him when he returns?"

Davis rocked himself, the woman's whispers haunting him.

"Davis!" Chaz said. "What do we do now?"

"We ..." Davis took a deep breath. *Just a dupe. She was just a dupe. In the real world, she's already dead.* "What would we do if we caught him, Chaz?"

"Interrogate him. Like we did earlier."

"Earlier, in the precinct and with the narco, we simply flashed our badges. But the Photographer already believes he's a dupe. I don't think it will work."

Chaz considered that.

"What we *really* need," Davis said, "is to pin down where the IRL cops can find him. He's obviously got a third hideout—the place where he really lives. If we can find that and send it to Maria, I think they'll have a good shot at grabbing him."

"So ..."

"So we watch him when he comes back," Davis said, taking a deep breath. "And we tail him. If it looks like he's spotted us, we capture him and see what we can beat out of him. Maybe that will be enough. But hopefully, instead we can find where he lives."

"Great, okay," Chaz said. "But we're not waiting here. Not with those corpses in there."

"We shouldn't go far, in case he—"

"You need a break, Davis. Look at you! Hell, *I* need a break. We'll go get a coffee or something. When's the last time we ate? Those burritos?" He thought for a moment.

"Better yet. We'll go to Ingred Street. It's four, right? Good timing."

Ingred. *Of course you want to go to Ingred.*

Davis just nodded his head, mute. Chaz was right. Though they probably should stake out nearby and watch, he was at his limit. He couldn't confront a killer like this. He needed some time to recover.

"Ingred it is," Davis said, standing.

Seven

Chaz left him, as he always did when they stopped at the park on the corner of Ingred and Ninth.

It was a little city park, of the type you found on neighborhood corners. Full of playsets that were old but sturdy, coated periodically in new layers of paint for a facelift. The place smelled better than the streets did. Of dirt and wet sand. Of course, it *sounded* better too. Over the distant rumbling of construction equipment and honking horns, here you could hear children.

Davis smiled, stepping up to the corner of the park, basking in the sounds of the laughter. Of children running, shouting, playing. When was the last time he'd just *enjoyed* life? He'd lost that skill, which seemed so natural to children. They didn't have to work at having fun.

Hal was there, as he'd hoped. Though he was eight, he seemed smaller than the kids he played with. A mop of dark hair, messy as always, and a ready smile. He was never happier than when he was around others. He liked people. He got that from his dad too. Davis had always thought that would make him a good cop.

Hal stopped in place when he saw Davis, then grinned widely. The worry that they might get back too late to catch the killer fled Davis's mind. Even with all the baggage that came along with visiting here, seeing Hal was worth it.

Hal ran up, and Davis grabbed him in a huge hug. The kid didn't ask why his father had come to see him on a random day, unannounced. He didn't connect that it was 16:00, when Davis knew his wife would be napping and the kid would be out playing. Hal was just happy he got to see his father.

And fortunately, court orders didn't cover dupes inside a Snapshot.

"Dad!" Hal said. "I haven't seen you in *forever*."

"I've been busy with work."

"Catching bad guys?"

"Catching bad guys," Davis said softly.

"Dad," Hal said. "We went to the *zoo*. I got a stuffed penguin. And there was a little antelope—it's called a dik-dik, but we're not supposed to laugh—and when we went walking, it *followed* me, Dad. It followed me all around. It attacked Greg. Kept butting its little head into his leg, everywhere he went, but it *liked* me."

Hal took a deep breath, then grabbed Davis in another hug. "Are you here to talk to Mommy?"

Davis glanced toward a window of her nearby apartment. The blinds were drawn.

"No," Davis said.

"Oh." Hal looked morose for a minute, then perked up. "Want to be a monster?"

"I'd love to be a monster."

The next hour was a bliss of chasing, growling, climbing on the jungle gym, and imagination. They were monsters, they were superheroes, they built mountains of sand and then stomped them. Hal changed the rules indiscriminately to every game as they played, and Davis wondered why he'd ever been annoyed at that. This kid didn't need more structure. He needed to be free, to live, to have all the things his father didn't have.

It didn't last though. It couldn't last. Eventually he spotted Chaz waiting for him at a nearby corner—and he couldn't believe that the time was over already. Sweating, Davis felt his grin melt away.

Right. The world waited; Chaz was its banner, held aloft to gather the faithful. Or in Davis's case, the reluctant.

Hal stepped up beside him. "Is that your partner?"

"Yeah," Davis said.

"You've gotta go?"

Davis pulled him close, and felt tears in his eyes. "Yeah." Then he turned, squatting down and fishing in his pocket. He took out the nickel, his fingers brushing past the paper with the number, and held it out. "Check it."

"Two thousand one?" Hal said. "Oh! You've been looking for one of these."

"Keep it," Davis said.

"Really?"

"Yeah," Davis said. "I've got another."

"You found *two*?"

The same one twice, he thought, then hugged his son one last time. Hal seemed to sense something to it, and clung tightly.

"Can't you stay a little longer?" Hal asked.

"No. Work needs me." *And your mother will be down soon.*

He forced himself to let go. Hal sighed, then ran off to show the nickel to one of his friends. Davis sat and pulled his shoes and socks back on, then trudged across the road toward Chaz.

It twisted him up inside. That hour had been wonderful, but the harsh reality was that this *wasn't* his son. The real Hal wouldn't remember this event, or the other dozen times that Davis had come to visit in the Snapshot. The real Hal would instead go on thinking that his father never visited.

"Not fair," Chaz said, hands in pockets. "You should be able to see him whenever you want, Davis."

"It's only temporary," Davis said.

"Temporary for *six months* now."

"We'll figure out custody soon. My wife—"

"Your ex-wife."

"—Molly is just protective. She's always been like that. Doesn't want Hal getting caught between us."

"It's still a raw deal," Chaz said. Then he sighed. "Food?"

"Sure." Time to deal with his memories of Hal would be welcome. Davis needed to recover, it seemed, from his break to recover.

They chose Fong's, a place around the corner that Davis had always liked. On the way in he froze, turning to look over his shoulder at someone who had just passed. Had that been . . . the woman from the diner?

No. Different clothing. Still, it left him thinking, clutching the number in his pocket. They went inside and were seated in a little booth by the window.

"Do you ever wish," Chaz said, "that we could just live in here? You know, in a Snapshot?"

"You're the one who's always reminding me it isn't real."

"Yeah," Chaz said, sipping the water the waitress brought. "But . . . I mean, do you ever wonder?"

"If it's exactly like the outside world," Davis said, "then what would be the point?"

"Confidence," Chaz said, staring out the window. "In

here . . . I just, I can do things. I don't worry as much. I'd like to be able to take that with me to the outside, you know? Or stay in here, let days pass, instead of switching the place off."

Davis grunted, taking a sip of his own water. "I'd like that."

"You would? I'm surprised."

Davis nodded. "I'd like to see what kind of difference I make," he said softly. "You know, we call them Deviations. Problems that *we* introduce into the system. But there's another way to look at them. Everything that changes in here, everything different, happens because *we* cause it. I'd like to see that run for a week. A month. A year."

"Huh. You think it would be better or worse than the real world in a year? Because of us."

"I don't know that I care," Davis said. "So long as it's different. Then I'd know I meant something." He fished in his pocket, got out the woman's number. "We don't let them live long enough in here to develop into distinct people."

"They're just dupes though."

They ordered. Davis got his favorite, cashew chicken. Chaz asked the waitress what the spiciest thing on the menu was, and ordered that. Then he asked for mustard to come with it.

Davis smiled, watching out the window. He'd hoped to catch a glimpse of Molly as she came to get Hal, but he couldn't spot the boy in the park. She'd fetched him already.

"Is it . . . always like this?" Chaz asked softly. "Police work. The things we saw back there."

"You weren't on any murder cases in Mexico City?"

Chaz shook his head. "I was a traffic cop there too. Never even saw a real car wreck; Mexico City had already outlawed manual-driving cars. Spent my time yelling at kids for jay-walking. That's why I kept pushing for transfers. I wanted to land somewhere I could actually be a *cop*."

Davis broke his chopsticks apart and rolled them together to clear the splinters. "Well," he said softly, "yes. Real police work was a lot like this. Except for the times when it wasn't, which was most days."

"There you go again," Chaz said, grinning. "Not making sense. Contradicting yourself."

"It always makes sense when I explain it, doesn't it?"

"I suppose."

"Being a cop, a detective on real cases, is mostly about boredom. Sitting around doing nothing, pushing paper, talking to people. Waiting. It's about *waiting* for something to go wrong. And when we get called, when we have something to do, it means that by definition we're too late.

"I always imagined serving justice, fixing problems. But most of the time we aren't saviors. We arrive in time to see someone dead, and maybe we catch the person who did it. But that doesn't matter to the people who were killed. For them we're really just . . . witnesses." He looked down. "I tell myself that at least *someone* was there."

They ate in silence. The cashew chicken wasn't as good as Davis remembered it being. Too salty. He spent the time staring at the woman's number.

I need something like this, he thought, turning it over in his fingers. Her number on one side. Death on the other—the address of the school. He flipped it back over. *I need a new start, in real life.*

He had to get over Molly. He *knew* he had to get over Molly. See other people. Even though he'd held out hope through the divorce.

But this number itself . . . it was a trap. He couldn't call a woman and lie to her, pretending he'd met her for real. It was a crutch. He just needed to change his life.

You're planning a change. Warsaw Street. He wouldn't have much time to get there after spying on the Photographer at 19:30.

"You going to call that?" Chaz asked as they finished up.

Davis turned it over again, then balled it up. "What's the point?" Davis said. "Let's go catch a bad guy."

He left the little slip of paper on the table beside his uneaten fortune cookie.

Eight

They got back to the school around 19:00, half an hour before the Photographer was supposed to return. They entered an apartment building with back windows looking out at the school—one of the few places to watch from. After knocking a few doors, they found an apartment where no one answered. Chaz kicked open the door, and Davis used his regular police badge—not his reality badge—to quiet the neighbors.

They settled down in the bathroom, where a tiny window gave them a good—if cramped—view. As they waited, Davis played with the facts, dancing them around in his head. As long as he could focus on those, on making neat rows of ideas—on grouping them into abstract sets and collections—he didn't feel so nervous.

"Why poison?" he finally said.

"Hmm?" Chaz asked, standing beside the toilet.

"He's killing them with what he sees as their flaws," Davis said. "He locked those poor people in with bees so their allergies would kill them. He suffocated the asthmatics. It's like . . . he sees himself as culling the species. Letting our own diseases or handicaps destroy us. The people who were paralyzed? The cops found bloody scrapes on the side of the half-full pool. People trying to climb out, breaking finger-nails. He dumped those poor people in a swimming pool alive, and let them drown because all their limbs didn't work."

"Bastard," Chaz whispered.

"Yeah. But the poison . . . Why the poison? For the far-sighted people? It doesn't fit the pattern." Davis tapped on the window, beside where the paint had chipped free. Outside, it was growing dark. "And another thing. Why in the *world* didn't the precinct tell us about this?"

"Maybe they worried we'd do what we're doing," Chaz said.

"Who cares though? Maybe we create a few more Deviations for a meaningless domestic abuse case, but wouldn't getting a clue about a terrible murderer be worth that risk? Besides, they know we usually ignore orders to go to saferooms—so we're out creating Deviations anyway. Might as well have us doing something useful."

"Yeah, but they call him the *Photographer*," Chaz said. "He knows about Snapshots and how to avoid them, right? That's what Maria said. We can't do anything to help."

"Like we're not doing anything now?"

"That's different. They don't realize you could actually do something—they think we're both useless, but you, you're *stealth competent*, Davis."

Davis grunted. "I don't buy it, Chaz. We did a Snapshot last week to find that kid working with the Juarez. Why not have us just pop over to that old apartment building? They'd have known about it IRL by then. We could peek in and see if any of the drowning people were still alive on that day—and that would have let us get some intel. But no, instead the precinct just pretends we can't do anything."

"Too deep for me," Chaz said. He pointed out the window. "I can tell you though, this stakeout feels wrong. What if he doesn't go in this way? What if he's been scared off, and doesn't come here at all? Or what if he returned early today, before we got back?"

"One of us should go in there, huh?" Davis said, feeling nervous.

"Yeah." Chaz glanced at him. "Don't worry. I'll do it."

"We should flip for it or something."

"Nah. I'm good." He patted Davis on the shoulder. "I'll text you once I get into position to watch the gym. I'll listen a little bit, then peek in and make sure he's not already in there. You text me if you see him approach. Okay?"

Davis nodded, taking a deep, relieved breath. Chaz walked to the door, but Davis called after him.

"Chaz?"

"Yeah, partner?"

"I couldn't pull the trigger."

Chaz frowned from the doorway. "What—"

"You wanted to know why I'm in here," Davis said, looking back out the window. "Years ago, when I was a real cop, we were in a shootout. Real bad guys, hostages, the terrible kind of stuff that ends up on the news. They sent in everyone. And I . . ."

"Couldn't shoot?"

"Had one right in my sights. And I blew it. You hear about Perez?"

"Yeah."

"The guy I couldn't shoot, he killed her. They found me trembling in the hallway, gun on the floor in front of me." He squeezed his eyes closed. "I thought . . . well, you should know."

"I already did."

"But—"

"Gutierrez told me," Chaz said. "Soon after I got assigned to you. I figured it was better if you told me yourself, you know? If I gave you a chance to bare your soul. Then we could be *real* partners."

Davis blinked, staring at the grinning taller man. *Here I think we're sharing something,* Davis thought, *and then you remind me how good you are at lying.*

"I'll text you," Chaz said, then left.

Davis waited, watching carefully while Chaz slipped across the street and into the building. They had time before the Photographer was supposed to return, but still Davis had visions of the killer spotting Chaz and bolting before either of them could catch him.

Shortly after Chaz entered the building, Davis's phone buzzed. He checked it, but was surprised to see the text wasn't from his partner.

Davis, Maria sent. She'd still be on duty, IRL. She worked a long shift on Snapshot days. *It's getting close to your second case. You guys in the saferoom?*

Yes, Davis sent back, trying to watch both the alley outside and his phone at once.

Good. You have the second case details. Head to Tenth. Be aware, there's going to be some gang violence one block over, at Warsaw Street. Advised to stay away from that. Just check on the domestic case on Tenth.

Understood, Davis sent.

He considered telling her what they were really doing, but decided against it. They'd never turned off the Snapshot while Davis and Chaz were in it, but he wouldn't put it past them. Of course, the two officers wouldn't be reclaimed with the dupes, but it would still be disconcerting to watch it all break down around him.

He stood with his thumb on the phone. For months after the incident where Perez had died, he'd berated himself for not being strong enough. After that, he'd started to berate himself for ever thinking he could shoot another human being. It wasn't in his nature, or it hadn't been.

He had a copy of his own record, nestled on his phone, hidden away behind a password. He'd taken it off Maria's computer at one point. So many commendations early on. *Great investigator. Knows people; he can make them talk when nobody else can. People trust him, even those who shouldn't.*

And then the incident.

Unfit for fieldwork. Severe anxiety. Recommended for therapy and, if retained, strongly recommended that he be put on Snapshot duty.

The others in the precinct hadn't used such sterile terminology about him. He still didn't know if Maria had claimed him for Snapshot duty because she'd thought his investigative skills would be put to good use here, or if she'd assumed that this place would teach him how to kill.

Here, Chaz finally sent. *No sounds from the pool locker room. Anything out there?*

No, Davis sent.

I'm going to peek in.

Davis waited, heart beating rapidly. What a fool he was. He didn't even have to be the one in danger for his nerves to go off!

He's not here, Chaz sent. *And nothing is disturbed. Let's hope he doesn't get spooked away permanently by the cops finding his last place.*

Yeah, Davis sent. *Be careful. If he doesn't go in this way, you'll have no warning.*

Roger.

And then, a moment later, the phone buzzed again.

If it were me in danger, Chaz sent, *you'd shoot.*

I can't say.

You would, Chaz sent. *I know it.*

Davis wasn't sure. Even still. People felt that being in a Snapshot lowered the stakes. But at the same time, all these people—they'd been created so that Davis and Chaz could solve their little cases. An entire city populated, then destroyed in a day. Millions wiped out. A periodic holocaust. If he failed, it was all for nothing.

Seemed like huge stakes to him.

Anything? Chaz sent.

No. I'll tell you if I see anything, Chaz. But if you keep distracting me— He stopped mid-sentence, and didn't send the text.

Someone was moving through the alleyway. A tall man in a long coat, his hands in the pockets. With the sun having set, there wasn't enough light to see him by, but he matched the profile.

Davis's heart leaped. *He's here,* he quickly texted.

Finally, Chaz sent.

Davis contained his breathing, trying not to imagine what would happen if the Photographer spotted Chaz. That wasn't likely to happen. Was it? But what if he checked the woman they'd shot, and found her with a bullet wound? Davis hadn't considered that.

The Photographer entered the building.

A short time later, Chaz sent, *He just passed me. Went into the pool area.*

At the very least, Davis didn't have to keep worrying about Warsaw Street. They had a new case, a more important one. They wouldn't be heading that way, and so none of his preparations would matter.

He found that idea comforting. Almost comforting enough to soothe his anxiety.

He's looking in the door to where the bodies are, Chaz texted.

You followed him into the locker room?

Yeah.

Stop texting me and stay safe, idiot!

Davis waited, tense, staring at his phone and feeling a

frustrating discordance. He'd just told Chaz not to update him—but that very silence put him on edge. He imagined his partner sneezing, the Photographer escaping. A dozen different scenarios.

He peeked in, Chaz sent, *at the bee room. Seemed very worried about insects escaping, even though they're all dead. It was dark in there though, and he doesn't seem to have noticed that the woman was shot. Maybe he was just listening to hear if they were still breathing. He closed the door quickly, then went on to look over his improvised pool of water. I'm back outside. He's eating a burger.*

Davis relaxed, pulling the lid down to sit on the toilet. Honestly, it might have been *less* nerve-racking to go in himself, rather than waiting out here.

A door opened nearby in the apartment. Damn. The people who owned this place were back. *I'm moving out to the street,* Davis sent. *So I can follow when he leaves.*

He pushed out of the bathroom, causing a woman to drop her groceries and scream. Davis flashed her his badge, then realized he'd grabbed the reality badge and felt guilty for using it so injudiciously. Like Chaz did. Well, whatever.

He hurried out into the hallway, leaving the woman to collapse on her couch, holding her chest. He ran down the steps and into the night, then placed himself at the mouth of the alleyway connecting the back of the school to the street.

He settled down on the ground next to some steps, head bowed, trying to look like just another of the many bits of human refuse that littered the city.

A text came a short time later. *He's moving again. Back out your way.*

So soon? Davis sent.

Yeah. He seems anxious. Just wanted to check things, I guess.

Wait a bit, Davis sent. *Then follow.*

Davis huddled there, proud at how calm his breathing was. When the Photographer passed him, he caught a good glimpse of his Asian features and black hair. Once the man was far enough ahead, Davis got to his feet and pursued silently.

He's heading east, Davis sent.

I'll go parallel, Chaz sent. *Through the alleyways.*

Roger.

As he followed, Davis began to feel a thrill. Perhaps this was what Chaz felt. He tried to think like his partner did. To him, this was all just a game. Couldn't Davis enjoy a game?

Then the Photographer turned right.

Davis stopped on the corner.

He just turned toward Warsaw, Davis sent, his thumbs moving almost of their own accord.

Roger.

Davis continued on, feeling as if he were being pulled in the wake of the killer. The farther he walked, the more *inevitable* he realized it was. Of course the killer would turn toward Warsaw. Of course everything hinged on this point. Davis couldn't have escaped it if he'd wanted.

Eventually, the Photographer turned up a set of steps into a townhouse in a row of old buildings pressed close to one another. They weren't abandoned, just well used. Most had shingles worn off the roofs, making them look balding.

They'd found the killer's real home. Davis stood there, looking up at it, bothered by how *normal* it seemed.

We're one street over from Warsaw, Davis thought. *Not on the side we were supposed to be on, for the domestic case.* That would be two blocks away.

Though this wasn't the exact same location where they would have gone if they hadn't picked up this case, it was still eerily close. Davis checked his phone. 20:00 exactly. Seventeen minutes away.

Chaz caught up to him. They stood together, looking up at the narrow townhouse.

"So, we send Maria this address?" Chaz asked. "We're done? They can go catch him here IRL?"

"I want more," Davis said softly.

"More?"

"I need to talk to him."

"I can go in and—"

"No," Davis said, shocked by how firm he felt. "Watch outside. Catch him if he runs."

"But—"

"Just do it, Chaz!" Davis said. "Stay out. Leave me alone." At least until 20:17 had passed.

The other man stepped back, surprised.

It isn't inevitable, Davis thought forcefully, walking up the steps. Was that how all the dupes felt? That their lives were their own? Never knowing that circumstances, replicated at the start of the day, would send them down exactly the same path?

He stepped up to the door, feeling his partner's eyes on his back. Chaz would have kicked in the front door.

Davis knocked.

Such a courteous request of a serial killer with blood on his hands, but there it was. Davis knocked again, politely.

The Photographer opened the door.

Nine

Even having heard the description and glimpsing the killer earlier, Davis found the man younger than he'd anticipated. He couldn't be more than twenty-two or twenty-three. So young to have caused so much horror in his life.

"What do you want?" the Photographer asked, looking Davis up and down.

Davis held up his reality badge.

The Photographer saw it, eyes widening. Then he smiled. "It's beautiful," he whispered.

"I need to—" Davis began.

The Photographer tried to slam the door. Davis got his foot between it and the frame, moving by instinct to block it from being shut. In the rush of the moment, he didn't even feel the pain. The Photographer turned and scrambled away.

"Davis!" Chaz called.

"Run around to the back door!" Davis shouted, shoving

into the townhouse. He didn't think. He was proud that he didn't tremble. Yes, maybe his time in the Snapshot *had* changed him.

Inside, the walls were painted a homey shade of peach and the wooden floors were bare and polished. The Photographer ducked around a corner, and his feet thumped up a set of stairs. Davis followed in a rush, yanking his gun out.

He passed suitcases set along the wall. Packed, a part of him noticed. *He's leaving. This address is useless. They'll find him gone IRL when they come here.* The Photographer had indeed been spooked by the cops finding the pool earlier.

Davis dashed up the steps. *Careful. Remember your training.*

At the top of the steps, he checked his corners—right, then left—to make sure nobody was standing there ready to ambush him. *Don't let the runner draw you into being careless. Be quick, but efficient. Control the situation.*

It was darker up here. No lights on. He continued forward, sweating, breathing in quick, sharp breaths. There were only two rooms in this hallway, which ended at a set of wooden steps pulled down from the ceiling, leading toward an attic.

Davis carefully checked one room, a bedroom, while trying to watch those steps ahead. The room was empty. He crossed the hallway and shoved open the other door, checking the corners.

No killer here either. But there was a captive.

An older Asian man sat on the ground, bound against the wall, weeping, with a gag over his mouth. On the floor in front of him was a series of cups that he'd barely be able to reach.

"I knew it," a voice called from the hallway outside. From the direction of the wooden steps. "I knew it was a Snapshot. Nobody ever believed me. But I knew you'd come someday."

Davis forced himself to ignore the captive. He stepped out into the hall again. The only light was what filtered up from the stairwell behind him, but it was enough to see that the hallway was completely normal. Pictures on the walls. A rug on the floor. The aroma of lemon-scented polish in the air.

And yet a kidnapped man wept to his right, and the icy voice of a madman floated down from the attic above.

Getting ready to flee out onto the roof maybe? Davis thought. These townhouses were built shoulder to shoulder; you could run across them. Davis would never chase down a younger man, in better shape, over that terrain.

"How did you know?" Davis called out, trying to think of something to stall the killer. "How did you figure out you were in a Snapshot?"

"The Deviations," the Photographer called back. Yes, he'd climbed those wooden steps. He was right up there.

Listening. "This life is too broken. Too many people gone wrong, too many neighborhoods left to rot. The Snapshot is . . . is falling apart. Too many Deviations."

"You're right," Davis called. "Yeah, I've noticed too. We can't let it happen. We've got to get rid of the Deviations, right? Keep the Snapshot stable?"

It was complete nonsense, but he could see how it might make sense.

"Why would you care?" the voice rasped.

"I'm part of it," Davis said. "This is my home."

The Snapshot is the only thing that is rational. Life is chaos the first time, but if you live it again, you see that it's very orderly. The system is too complex for us to figure out on the fly. But if I could live here, I could always know what was coming. . . .

"No. You're from outside. You're a cop."

"Doesn't mean I can't agree with you," Davis shouted. "I can help you keep this place together. Make the Snapshot run. It needs to run, right? I have to keep it together, keep it from crumbling, so I can do my job."

It seemed like the right thing to say, and remarkably it seemed to work. To an extent. The Photographer didn't run. He shuffled up above.

"You're a cop," he finally repeated. "You're here to stop me."

"Not you," Davis said. "No, not you. If we were in the real

world, I'd have to stop you. But we're not, are we? All I care about is keeping this place running. You're doing that. You're important. You're the only one who has figured it out. You can help me. Help me cleanse this place."

The Photographer started down the steps, but stopped on them, frozen. Uncertain. Davis felt sick, a striking nausea, as the man turned and started back up the steps.

"Wait!" Davis said. "Wait! I can prove it. I . . ." He trailed off, then stepped backward, looking into the room with the tied-up captive. The man reached his hands toward him, wrists bound, eyes pleading.

"I'll prove it!" Davis whispered.

Just a Snapshot. Not real. This is the only way to save people who are real. Don't be a coward. . . .

In a trance, Davis raised his gun at the man.

I can't do this. I can't. . . .

He'd already done it before with the push of a button. Hundreds of times. Every time he turned this place off.

He shot the man.

The gunshot broke the air. It was louder than he'd expected, and he winced. The man he'd shot slumped backward. This time the bullet had come out the back of the head, painting the wall.

His phone buzzed. He ignored it. He just stared at the dead man, then dropped his gun, shocked at himself.

"Did . . ." the Photographer's voice called. The man started back down the wooden steps. "Did you just do it?"

"Got to . . . got to protect the Snapshot," Davis said, his voice trembling. He squeezed his eyes shut.

"You know them for what they are," the Photographer said, sounding proud. "But you should know, we're not supposed to kill them. We let the Snapshot do it, like the immune system of the body. Clear them out."

The Photographer walked up to him. "That one, my uncle, he can't see. We wait until he's thirsty, then let him pick a drink. But he can't read the labels. So the system kills him."

"I'll do it right next time," Davis whispered. "What's the plan? Who is next? I can help."

The Photographer licked his lips. "I'm running out of people I can find on the street," he said. "We've got to be careful though. The cops from inside will try to stop us. They don't understand."

"I do."

"Mary Magdalene School," the Photographer said. "Seventeen children have peanut allergies. I've been working out how to do it, so we can be hidden. But if you're with me, if the cops outside the Snapshot don't care, then maybe I don't have to worry. Either way, we move on May twelfth. I've found out that—"

A gunshot went off: loud, arrogant, unexpected. The

Photographer dropped like a puppet with its strings cut. Davis turned to see Chaz at the top of the steps, lit from below, gun in hand.

"Holy hell!" Chaz said. "Davis, you all right? How'd he disarm you?"

Davis blinked. *Chaz, you idiot.*

His phone buzzed a long buzz. The alarm.

20:17 on the dot.

Davis calmly picked up his gun. They were a distance from Warsaw, but he'd have to go forward with his plan anyway. It would work, right? It was plausible?

Did he care?

Chaz shoved past Davis and knelt by the killer. "Wow. He's just a kid." He looked up into the room with the dead man. "Hell! What happened, Davis?"

In response, Davis raised his gun and pointed it at Chaz's head.

Chaz stumbled back. "Davis?"

"Goodbye, Chaz."

"Whoa. Whoa, Davis! What are you doing!"

"Tell me," Davis said softly. "When you go see Molly in the Snapshot, do you have to seduce her anew each time? Or do you flash your badge, convince her she's not real, and just take her that way?"

Chaz's jaw dropped, his eyes wide.

"You do it so quickly," Davis said. "Every time I visit Hal, right?"

"Davis, think about this!"

"I *have* thought about it, Chaz!" Davis shouted. "You see this gun? This *is* me thinking about it!"

Outside, distantly, gunfire went off. The gang violence on Warsaw.

"This gun," Davis snapped, "came from evidence, IRL. Those shots you hear—someone is using this gun right now to fire on another gang member. I thought, how to disguise a murder in the Snapshot? I could use the same gun we *know* a gangster had. I could shoot you. Claim it was a stray bullet, and the ballistics will back me up. Nobody will know. They'll think it was an accident."

"Hell," Chaz whispered. Then he sighed and dropped his gun. "I guess you have thought about it."

Davis held his own gun, palms sweaty, teeth clenched. For once he wasn't nervous. For once he wasn't trembling, or breathing quickly. He was *angry*. Furious.

"My wife, Chaz," he whispered.

"Your *ex*-wife."

"You think that makes it all right?"

Chaz shrugged. "No. Probably not." He closed his eyes.

Here we are. Need to do it quickly. Davis wiped his brow, gun arm steady.

And then . . . then he thought about second chances. About pretty smiles, about his son.

You were just thinking earlier about how you need to get over Molly, a piece of him whispered. *If you let her force you to do this, then what are you?*

Still, he'd just shot a man. An innocent man. Now here he was, with Chaz, at exactly the right moment. Just like he'd planned and imagined it. Why not take this step?

It was all inevitable, wasn't it?

Was it inevitable that he'd failed before, IRL? Was he the Deviation, or was Chaz? Did it matter?

I can *start fresh,* he thought. *Get a new life. Date new people. But if I pull this trigger, I'll never be able to do that. I'll never be able to live with myself if I kill him.*

He took a deep breath. In the end, people became cops because they wanted to do something good. At least that was what they told themselves. That was what he'd always told himself.

Davis lowered his gun.

Ten

How long have you known?" Chaz asked, raising a shot of whiskey to his lips. They were in the kitchen of the small townhouse, the one with two corpses upstairs.

"I caught sight of you up in the window about five months back," Davis said softly. "After that, it was obvious. You kept prompting me to go see Hal."

Davis poured himself another shot, and had to be careful not to spill, with his hand shaking. How could Chaz drink so calmly?

"I did it once in real life, Davis," Chaz said, leaning on the counter. "Shouldn't tell you that, should I? But I need to come clean. It was just before the divorce started."

Davis closed his eyes.

"That's why it works in the Snapshot," Chaz continued. "I don't show my badge. She thinks it's the second time, each time. I promised to come see her again, but never did, IRL.

I figured I needed to confine it to this place. Out of respect for my partner, you know? It's a Snapshot. Nothing matters in a Snapshot."

"Yeah," Davis said, then opened his eyes. "To nothing mattering." He raised his shot glass.

Chaz nodded, raising his own.

Davis drank and looked at his phone, which sat in front of him, the text he'd sent to Maria glowing on the screen.

Photographer, the serial killer, it read, *is going to try to kill a group of peanut-allergic children from Mary Magdalene School. Tomorrow, May 12th. Set up a sting, catch him. You can find evidence of his activities at the following addresses.* He'd then sent the address of the school and the house they were in now, hoping the evidence there would corroborate his words, even if the Photographer had moved on from them IRL.

Maria hadn't responded, but the message had gone through. He could imagine her shock. And her likely anger.

"We did good, partner," Chaz said. "Didn't we? We're going to do great things together moving forward."

"Chaz?"

"Yeah."

"I never want to see you after today. *Never again.*"

Chaz looked down at his empty glass. "Right. Okay."

They drank in silence.

"I'm glad you didn't shoot," Chaz eventually said. "Glad you couldn't shoot."

Davis finished his whiskey. "You know why I insist on turning off the Snapshot myself, each evening?"

"No. Why?"

"Every time I do it, I kill Hal. *Every time.* Someone has to do it, so I do it myself. But it rips me up each time, knowing. And if I've killed my son a hundred times, do you really think I couldn't shoot you?"

Chaz went white.

Together, they took their things and walked to the front of the building. Outside, the air smelled sweet, a breeze coming in off the ocean. Davis climbed down the steps, exhausted, then stopped at the bottom. A couple of people were on the street here. A tall black man. And a woman. The woman from the diner. She *had* changed her outfit.

"Detectives Davis and Chavez?" the tall man asked. "Can we have a word with you?"

Davis shared a look with Chaz, who shrugged.

"What's this about?" Davis asked. "You from the precinct?" His frown deepened. "You're from IRL? Are you feds?"

"We'll explain," the tall man said, taking Chaz by the shoulder, leading him a little farther down the street. The woman stepped up to Davis.

She was pretty. Like he remembered. "I lost your number," he blurted out. "Sorry."

She blushed. "Detective Davis. Why didn't you kill your partner today?"

"How do you know—"

"Please just answer the question."

Davis rubbed his chin. "Because I'm not a monster. Pointing the gun at him was a momentary lapse."

"A momentary lapse?" she asked. "That you planned for months, waiting for an exactly perfect Snapshot, where you would be able to hide your actions and pretend a gangster shot him?"

Farther down the street, Chaz suddenly shoved back from the tall man. "No!" Chaz shouted. "No, no, *no!*" He reached for his weapon.

The tall man calmly gunned Chaz down in the street.

Davis stared, feeling cold. *It can't be.*

"It would really help our investigation," the woman said, "if you could tell us what we did wrong."

"You're Snapshot detectives too," Davis said. "It . . . Damn! *That's* why they don't have us on the Photographer case. They're using someone else!"

"You're a distraction, Davis. A way to cover up the real teams, who come into the Snapshot on different days from you. We can file your records though, and show the city is using the Snapshot device that people paid for. We can pretend that we're not—"

"Doing something deeper," Davis said. "With secret cops. Watching people. Damn! That's why they don't want us working real cases, at least not the in-depth ones." He shivered, then continued, whispering. "Right now, you're here to investigate *me*. Today's a Snapshot . . . It's *a Snapshot of a Snapshot*."

"We weren't sure if it would work. No cop has ever before needed to be investigated for killing his partner in a Snapshot."

"But I didn't kill him."

"You did, in real life." She pointed. "After stopping the Photographer, you shot your partner."

"My plan—"

"Was clever, but you were too far from Warsaw. Maria found Chavez's death suspicious. You confessed under pressure, but then recanted, and a judge threw out the testimony. Now we need to catch you doing it, but we failed. Why?"

"Help you incriminate me?"

She shrugged.

"You really *don't* know how this works." He paused. "You're new, aren't you?"

"Newly promoted. You weren't deemed important enough

for the other two teams. They thought we could learn from this. And the classes say—"

"The classes won't replace living it," Davis said, numb. "You shouldn't have given me your number."

"So that *was* it," the man said, stepping up to them, leaving Chaz dead in the street. "I told you."

"I had to do *something*," the woman said. "He spotted me paying attention to him! It would have been weirder if I hadn't responded at all."

"No," Davis said. "You gave me something physical—that slip of paper. That created a persistent Deviation, and it changed me." He raised his hand to his head. "It changed what I did. *I* didn't choose. *You* made me choose. . . ."

The two nodded to each other. Then they started to walk off.

"Wait!" Davis said. "The Photographer! Did they get him?"

The man frowned. "Well, that case really is above your clearance—"

"Hell with that!" Davis said. "You're going to turn this all off in a moment. Tell me. *Did they get him?*"

"Yes," the woman said. "The information you sent from inside the Snapshot proved accurate. They caught him trying to contaminate food supplies at the school."

Davis closed his eyes and sighed. So he had done something. But not him. The other him.

He opened his eyes. "I'm the Deviation," he said. "But I'm the one who *didn't* kill my partner. I'm a better man than the one you have in custody, but I'm the one you're going to kill."

The woman looked apologetic. How could you *apologize* for destroying a whole city? For murdering a man, for murdering *him*?

"At least show me," he said.

"Show you?"

"The badge," Davis said. "Mine looks just like a metal shield. Prove it to me."

The woman reluctantly got out her wallet. "Yours looks like a shield to you because, in the day we're copying, that's what you saw. It has to be re-created exactly—"

"I know the mechanics of it. *Show me.*"

She held up the badge.

In it, Davis saw his life. A child. A young man. An adult. He saw Molly, good times and bad. He saw Hal's birth, and saw himself holding the boy. He saw tears, rage, love, and panic. He saw himself huddled in a shopping mall, in the middle of a nervous breakdown, and he saw himself standing firm, gun pointed at Chaz's head. He saw a hero and a fool. He saw everything.

And he knew. He knew he was fake. Up until that moment, he hadn't really believed.

He blinked, and it faded. The other two were already

walking away. They'd leave through a doorway that dupes couldn't see.

Davis walked over and sank down beside Chaz's dead body. "I guess you got it one way or another, partner."

The two detectives suddenly vanished ahead. No need for stealth in leaving—not when they were about to turn the Snapshot off.

"I pulled the trigger," Davis said. "When I needed to. So I guess the Snapshot did change me, eh, partner?" He sighed a long, deep sigh. "I wonder what it feels like when—"

Postscript

It's probably easy to guess that I'm fond of detective stories. *Legion* and *Dreamer* both have their roots in this genre, and you can find hints of it in my epic fantasy as well—whether it be Vasher searching for clues in Warbreaker, or Gawyn trying to track down a killer in the Wheel of Time.

At the same time, this is a genre that's been around since Poe—so a *lot* has been done with it already. I always want to find something that I can add to the conversation, rather than just copying things that have come before.

I'd say that the core of *Snapshot* was the desire to tell a multi-layered story, with different layers of reality matching different layers of crimes being planned. The first and coolest idea for me was that of a detective planning to kill his partner while at the same time investigating a different murder.

This story didn't start with a superhero/villain as the

(magical) origin of the Snapshot technology. Originally, it was just a far-future story where the technology had been developed. I really loved the idea of going into a replication of a day in the past to investigate crimes. It felt very classic cyberpunk to me, with some nice Philip K. Dick vibes as well.

Unfortunately, the story ended up having a huge problem. I needed this fantastic, amazing technology—but at the same time, couldn't progress the society too far. I couldn't let this story be diverted by bizarre, far-future worldbuilding or cultures. That would draw it too far away from the personal story between two detectives that I wanted to tell. (Beyond that, the Snapshot idea was already strange enough. If the world they investigated in was too weird, then I felt the story wouldn't have any grounding.)

Early readers, Peter and Moshe (my editors) included, identified this issue as their main hang-up in the story. Why did most of the technology seem like this was only a few years in the future? Surely if they had the technology to create a city from raw matter, they're post-scarcity, even post-singularity. It just didn't gibe. There were too many potential extrapolations of the science presented. If you can do things like create a Snapshot, why waste it on solving crimes? Why not create fantastical worlds to live in?

We needed the story to be near-future instead, with a normal technological curve—except for one or two hyperfantastical pieces of technology. And that felt exactly like something I'd already done, with the Reckoners. Changing this from a scientific origin to instead a fantastical (superhero) one solved this problem.

This is the sort of thing I talk about when I explain to readers the difference between what I perceive as a science fiction writer (someone who tries to realistically extrapolate the future) and a fantasy writer (someone who comes up with an interesting effect to explore, then justifies it with worldbuilding).

In the end, both are trying to explore what it means to be human. One starts with what we have, and works forward to reach something interesting, then extrapolates the ramifications. The other starts with the interesting thing, then asks how this could have come about. That's obviously not a catch-all definition, but it has worked for me as one way to explore the genres.

Anyway, Snapshot turned out very well. I'm particularly fond of the subtle intertwining of the three investigations: Chaz and Davis hunting the serial killer, the reader's growing understanding of what Davis is planning, and the other Snapshot detectives investigating Davis. These overlap with the three timelines. The Davis/Chaz timeline, the future they think they're from, and the future beyond that that the real detectives are from.

In reading this, I assume that the reader is going to guess that Davis himself isn't real. (The protagonist turning out not to be real is a staple of this genre—from *Blade Runner* to *The Sixth Sense*.) My goal is to use that twist as the one the reader is expecting, so that when Davis raises the gun to kill Chaz, you're completely blindsided—because you've been focused all along on the question of whether or not Davis is real. I wish I'd been able to reverse the surprises, so the one you're expecting (that he's not real) comes first, and *then* you're hit with the deeper twist, that he's planning to kill his partner. (And did kill his partner, in the real timeline.)

This never worked in my plotting or outlining, so I had to be satisfied with the current order of events, which I do think works. Particularly because I could end with the lights going out mid-sentence.

Brandon Sanderson